INSYNN

Loren Walker

Octopus & Elephant Books
PROVIDENCE, RHODE ISLAND

Octopus & Elephant Books
www.oandebooks.com

Publisher's Note: This is a work of fiction. Names, characters, places, and incidents are a product of the author's imagination. Any resemblance to actual people, living or dead, or to businesses, companies, events, institutions, or locales is completely coincidental.

Book Layout ©2015 BookDesignTemplates.com.

Cover by Deranged Doctor Designs.

INSYNN / Loren Walker. -- 1st ed.
ISBN 978-0-9973922-5-8

Contents

For the ones that I love.

PART ONE

When Iyo Sava died, and his grandson was declared his successor, a hundred meetings took place in the city of Lea. Shaky alliances formed, and arguments went through the night on whether or not action would, or should, take place. The grandson wasn't a true Sava, the men and women grumbled; for years he existed on the outskirts, taking advantage of his family's connections and wealth, always at a distance, holding no loyalty to anyone. It didn't matter what the old man wanted, the arguments repeated, or that there was only one surviving blood relative. The shift in leadership would ruin them all.

Theron Sava knew all this, because every conversation was reported back to him. His advisor, Bianco, came to his apartment every morning, ready with fresh gossip and the day's schedule. True to his character, Bianco needed no prodding. As soon as he cleared the threshold, Bianco launched into his updates: another gathering in West Lea, another muttered wave of threats, followed by half-hearted plans to appeal, to confront, to challenge the appointment at the end of the month.

"But nothing concrete," Bianco always added at the end, as if that fact was soothing. "Of course, they know better."

True enough. People might make threats, but no one would dare to directly challenge Theron, not with Bianco assigned to his care. It was the only reason why Theron hadn't been attacked at night or assassinated yet. Appointed by Iyo Sava, with the task of guiding Theron's succession, Bianco was known for his strict adherence to code and his undying loyalty to the Sava name. Most of his hair was gone, save for his white-flecked brows, which loomed over still-piercing black eyes. His face was slack with age, he had a double chin that wobbled when he spoke, and a comfortable belly over his trousers, but his hands were thick and calloused and he was known for using them if he felt disrespected, even at his age.

Anyone else would be grateful for the protection, Theron thought. *I'd rather have a fight.*

But he said nothing as Bianco rattled off names, times and places, pushed at him to get ready; they would be late, for goodness sake's, and he wasn't even dressed yet, cajoling Theron like a child, huffing and sighing.

It was easier, for now, to play along.

There were meetings all day, meetings in every borough of the capital city: meetings with old, grizzled heads of families; offended upstarts who needed their egos soothed; eager businesses looking to earn a place on their protection list. More than once, Theron wondered if any of them suspected how damp he was underneath his tailored suit, how his heart thrummed, how his mind raced, composing the words milliseconds before he opened his mouth. Did they all do the same?

Other times, he felt foolish for even caring what they thought. Close up, the Sava Syndicate was pathetic, really, a bunch of small-scale operators that focused on the black market, underground smuggling in mekaline, fuel cells and other illegal goods. The syndicate held influence in the industrial North, parts of the East coastline, and throughout Lea: construction companies, dock loading enterprises, restaurants, all covers to obscure revenue and redistribute. When Keller was the heir, the syndicate was moving into robberies, security breaches, corrupting public officials. Now that Keller was dead, business had plateaued, and everyone was looking for direction.

It should be easy to dismantle the whole system. He just couldn't figure out how.

And it wouldn't happen as long as Bianco remained so close, peering into his eyes like a paranoid mother, asking if he saw lights, or colors, or felt like he needed to sit down.

His seizures: his ongoing curse. Brain damage as a child that never healed, was never managed with any combination of medication. Being so close to Theron's grandfather, Bianco knew about every experimental treatment and drug regimen, and all the subsequent failures.

Still, one morning not long after his grandfather's death, a man appeared at Theron's door, visibly nervous, carrying a leather satchel, the smell of antiseptic about him. A doctor. A miracle cure.

Theron sighed. "My advisor sent you," he said bluntly, without introducing himself. "You're here to cure me."

"Well," the man stammered. "I'm here to help, sir. I understand that -"

"It's unnecessary," Theron cut him off. "So whoever calls to check on the results? Tell them there's nothing you can do."

"Going by the files forwarded, you haven't been evaluated in over ten years. There have been a lot of advancements in research, Mr. Sava, many treatment options."

"Brain damage is brain damage," Theron said through his teeth, hating every second of this conversation.

"Yes, of course," the doctor demurred. "But I must at least attempt to correct your condition."

Sure you do, Theron thought, staring hard at the man. *And your life is dependent on making me appear stronger, healthier, a worthy leader.* Bianco's rough hands were all over this.

Still, when the man was finished, and the door clicked shut behind him, Theron ordered a cease and desist notice sent to the doctor's clinic. He didn't have the time to empathize with the man's situation.

In the evenings, Theron went to parties and charitable functions. He shook hands, he nodded in conversations, he used some standard lines of intimidation or indifference, and even threw in a scripted joke now and again. He worked to remember to stand up straight so there would be no sudden slap on his back from Bianco, that friendly reminder to stop slouching. Be proud of your size, Bianco was always telling him. Slumped over like that, you look like a boy. Be a man. Shoulders back.

If he wasn't at a party, Theron was on a date. Bianco arranged dinners with beautiful women every week: girls of every height and weight and color, beautiful eyes, poignant profiles, slim and ethereal, soft and curvaceous, all tucking their hands into his elbow, flashing their heirloom jewelry, talking about families and religion and the latest in entertainment news. He went through all the routines of engagement, and they were always willing, their hands roving, their chests pushed out, watching for his response. But the ones who stuck around quickly grew sick of him. They were bored of how much he worked, how quiet he was, how he wasn't interested in mekaline or reckless behavior, how he wouldn't start a fight or threaten someone's life in their honor. They never knew what he was thinking, they never knew how he felt about anything. Theron heard every variation of the word "cold" thrown at him. He didn't stop them from leaving. Another candidate was always ready to take their place. As Bianco believed, it was important to show the world that Theron was a 'regular, hot-blooded man, who loved beautiful women.'

After the fourth woman severed her connections, Bianco confronted Theron in the town car. As the bodyguard, Grey, waited outside, Bianco placed his fingertips together and asked Theron if he was a homosexual.

"And if I were?" Theron shot back.

"If you are, so be it," Bianco said. "But you need a woman to create a family, whether she is your wife or your employee."

Theron rolled his eyes, sinking into the cushions.

Bianco puffed out his chest. "What's the matter with you? Don't you want to pass on the blood of your father and your grandfather, and all those before them?"

No, Theron thought. *I damn sure do not.*

But the man kept pushing. "Do you want to grow old alone?"

Theron slammed his hand against the door, a hard *thwack!*

Grey turned at the sound, peering through the tinted window.

But Bianco's eyes glinted. "Good to see a little fire in you."

It made Theron want to punch him. He held down the urge as Bianco knocked on the window, gesturing for Grey to open the door.

"Get some rest," he told Theron. "Busy day tomorrow. Be ready at eight."

Theron's apartment was on the forty-seventh floor, in a silver skyscraper, nestled in the city's most exclusive neighborhood. His grandfather bought the place before he died, the deed placed in Theron's name, already furnished in traditional dark colors, heavy fabrics and leather. When he opened the door and caught the familiar scent, Theron half-expected the old man's ghost to be there, smacking Theron across the back of the head, uttering that familiar growl: "I knew you couldn't be trusted with anything important."

Theron kept the lights off as he shrugged out of his suit jacket, undershirt and trousers. He left them where they lay, the soft swish of fabric the only indication of where they landed. Then he removed the gold ring from his middle right finger, and laid the gold Sentry pistol next it. Other Savas kept their rings on, even when they slept, to their custom-made handguns could always work for them, and only them, should danger arise in the night. But Theron was glad to shed both items from his person.

Finally, Theron took out five black cubes from the desk by the window. He rotated them in his fingers, like a juggler, as he took a seat in his leather chair.

In moments away from Bianco and the bodyguard, Theron had bought five Lissomes, those communication and research devices available in vending machines throughout the city. He set them on the edge of his desk carefully, lined up four inches apart. Then, with five quick flicks of his hand, the Lissomes were activated. Only hours remained until eight in the morning, and there was so much to monitor, so much to push forward. He dove into the light of the pixels before him.

Theron was in the process of establishing a manufacturing company in the North, near the city of Daro. It wasn't so unusual in his field: the Sava Syndicate held over a hundred businesses, serving as fronts. His would be one of many, glanced at, but unacknowledged, just as he wanted. Publicly, the company would produce the trinkets he invented: the shock-absorbing gloves for martial arts sparring, for example. But internally, the business would specialize in defensive equipment. HALOs to start, those half-circles of metal that could disrupt telepathy and other psychic transmissions. People would buy them in droves when the story of the NINE became public knowledge. That day was coming soon. He would be ready for it.

But before he could start production, Theron needed full ownership of the HALO. The headgear was developed in tandem with Renzo Byrne, a week of tossing around ideas, soldering, shaping and chip installation. Fair was fair. Renzo was co-designer. Theron wanted to be professional about it.

A month ago, he'd sent formal paperwork to Renzo, with a generous offer to buy the HALO design outright. Then again, two weeks ago. Still no response. For the moment, Theron chose not to push. He was still too angry with Renzo and the rest of his family to make direct contact. He could always send someone, if needed, to press the issue.

As he worked, he brought up an audio recording. Voices rippled through the Lissome's soundsystem, alternating between his own quiet questions and Kuri Nimat's choking, desperate replies. The sessions were now so familiar that Theron could mouth every question and response.

"Why bribe Sydel for money?"

"To extract the implant.... We were desperate.... Shantou was getting worse...."

"Why did she deteriorate, and not you?"

"It was a mistake...."

"Tell me what you did."

"We snuck into a medlab, we bribed the technician... but we didn't know there was metal inside our heads.... the MRI on Shantou, the magnetism.... it ripped through her brain, she was screaming...."

"What does the metal implant do?"

"I don't know.... please, I don't know...."

"Where is Shantou now?"

"I can't.... I won't tell you...."

"Did you kill Yann Qin?"

"Not on purpose.... I just wanted to talk...."

"Why leave me and my cousins alive? Why not kill us, along with our parents?"

"I was scared.... I was young, I just wanted you to forget that you'd seen us .... I didn't mean to hurt anyone...."

Theron stopped the recording. Opening another drawer, he removed a tiny plastic bag, and turned it over in his palm.

Barely a millimeter wide and one-inch-long, the needle had no discerning features.

"It's been in there for years," the surgeon had told him weeks ago, eying the item with interest. "Some sort of industrial accident?"

Theron had said nothing, his hand outstretched. The examiner dropped the needle from the tweezers into Theron's gloved palm. Before him, Kuri Nimat's corpse lay on its stomach, the back of its skull was opened, bloodless, surrounded by wet tools.

Twenty-five years, Theron thought, holding the needle between his thumb and forefinger. The metal caught the moonlight. He still didn't understand what it was, but he would soon, when he found the right person to take it apart and examine it.

Patience. The information was out there, somewhere. And so were the rest of the NINE, who presumably had the same implants in their skulls.

The NINE. A group of strangers, brought together for an underground experiment, who left as powerful psychics, who killed most of Theron's family, and then disappeared into the world twenty-five years ago. Even with all his research, Theron still couldn't figure out why. Why did the NINE kill his parents, his aunt and uncle, but leave him and his cousins alive? How did they go into their brains, skew their memories, their personalities, so none of them were ever the same? Theron had been left with frequent seizures, but he was mostly the same person. But Kadise, Keller and Xanto, they were different after the NINE, so cruel, unable to process sympathy. Of course, given that they were blood members of the Sava crime syndicate, their cruelty was seen as a positive, and Theron's condition as weakness. But now he was the only one left alive. The last one who cared enough to find out the reason why, and to ensure that it never happened again.

The night stretched on, the black turning to blue. Finally, sleep knocked on the back of Theron's head, unable to be ignored any longer. He'd trained himself years ago to need little to no rest. Just a couple of hours, and he could put on the mask again.

Rising, Theron turned to stand in front of the great bay window, the centerpiece of the apartment. He'd jimmied open the glass on the first night he moved in. The design didn't include air from the outside, but he figured out how to pop it from the frame and put it back into place every morning, so Bianco wouldn't see it. It was routine now, he couldn't expect to sleep without the process. When the window was open, every night offered the rush of possibility.

Reminding him that the end was in sight.

Theron held a weekly appointment with his cousin, Jetsun Sava, at her law offices in Upper Lea. Jetsun was his lawyer, his second cousin, and in some fashion, his friend. She was dismissive, and abrupt, and far too concerned about her beautiful blonde exterior, but she held onto secrets. As far as he could tell, she had never disclosed his risky interactions with the Byrne family to anyone.

"Another dramatic breakup, I hear," Jetsun murmured, poring over the registration paperwork. With her free right hand, she typed like she was playing the piano: wrists arched, her fingers flying in a pattern, maintaining his world.

When Theron shrugged, Jetsun just smirked. "So cool and smooth about it. Aren't you different since Ges. Have you seen her lately? She's got three kids now, but she's just as snotty-looking as ever. Looks like she's aged twenty years. Not very attractive."

"Thanks, Jet," Theron said flatly. It wasn't news to him. Over the past ten years, he'd seen Gesminna a few times. The last time, she had only two children, both black-haired, blue-eyed and sullen; she was married off to some lower syndicate boss in Lea. That memory of deceit that used to wrench him, though, was hardly a pinprick now. Progress. Or maybe just numbness, after so long.

Jetsun leaned back in her chair, her nails tapping on the handrail. "You still hung up on that girl?"

"Gesminna?"

"You know who I mean."

He did. But he didn't acknowledge it.

Jetsun tossed her head back, shaking out the blonde waves. "Should I make some inquiries? In case you're feeling lonely?" she drawled.

"No." It was easier to remain curt.

Jetsun sighed, a low, musical hum.

"Yes, indeed," she murmured. "You've certainly changed. I hardly recognize you."

Good.

He kept that remark to himself.

* * *

Theron Sava spent his first twenty years as a slave to his infatuations: he fell in love, hard and fast, with a dozen different girls. Everyone knew who his family was, and his cousins thrived on the attention and fear, but Theron wished for another life. Maybe that was why he was so quick to fall.

But his intentions always backfired. He gave the wrong gift, he said the wrong thing and the girl made it public, so the teasing began anew and he was freshly humiliated. Very quickly, Theron learned to not even acknowledge any hint of desire. It was better to remain in the shadows and pine, instead of pursue. Why bother? He already knew the outcome.

When he was twenty-two, and starting to take part in business deals, Gesminna Ferri was introduced to him: a local socialite, good family, involved in charity work. He was no good at talking to women, or anyone, really. Every conversation was strangled, him panicked on the inside, rehearsing every line, but the words spoken always the opposite of his intention. Ges didn't seem to mind, though. Then she asked him to take her out for dinner.

They looked good together, everyone thought so. Ges said he was handsome, though Theron was always quick to deny the compliment; he'd been called ugly so many times growing up, he'd never believe otherwise. But she was beautiful, and she knew it by the way she swung her hips in front of him. Black hair, pale blue eyes, clear copper skin, slim and elegant and cool. She didn't mind his frequent, awkward silences, or when he had to disappear for days on end. She didn't mind his sweating palms, or how he fumbled in the dark with her blouse that first time. With her, he was always careful when it came to his seizures and the warning signs: the aura, the haze, the quickening of his heart, all clues to excuse himself and find the nearest washroom, or at least a quiet alcove to brace his body against.

But one day, it hit too fast. When he came out of it, servants had surrounded him, clucking with fear and sympathy. But Ges was also standing over him.

"It's not -" he began in a panic, even as his head was spinning. "I'm not - "

"I'm not upset," she interrupted him. There was a strange, pinched expression on her face. He couldn't tell what it was: fear, or disgust, or just incomprehension.

An awkward silence followed, until the servants started to clean up the broken vase on the floor. Ges didn't crouch down next to him. She just waited until he got to his feet. Only then did she take his arm.

The next day, a seizure disorder specialist was at his door. The doctors couldn't do anything more for him, he already knew that, but he went through the tests, the blood withdrawals, the puzzled results, for her.

After six months, he proposed marriage. She said yes. He was in a state of bliss for days, floating through the motions.

Then his cousin Jetsun came to his apartment in Lea, on a break from law school. Theron had barely closed the front door before she announced, "You need to know about something. And it's going to hurt."

His heart gave one hard thump. *The dream ends*, he thought immediately. *Too good to be true.*

"I saw Ges on the Express train, all over some man. Everyone saw. She wasn't even trying to hide it."

Of course she wasn't.

"I knew it," Jetsun muttered. "I could tell from the start, what a phony she was."

One phony to another.

Suddenly, Jetsun's face was in front of his, pink and furious. "She's embarrassing you in public," she spat each word. "Do something about it."

Like what?" Theron shot back. He leaned against the wall, his head in his hand, wishing he could press his skull hard enough to erase all memory of this moment.

"If you don't do something, I will."

"Don't make threats on my behalf," Theron snapped. "It's none of your business.

"Fine," Jetsun said. "Be a cuckold. See if I care. I try to warn you, get it tossed back in my face, because you're too much of a coward to do anything."

Theron threw an ashtray at her. It crashed through the door's fine glass design. The wind sucked through the hole, making a howling, haunting sound. Jetsun gaped at him, face white with surprise. Then she flounced out of the apartment, kicking aside the broken glass.

She was right. He was a coward. It took a full day to summon the courage to confront Gesminna. She shrugged when he asked her why, her eyes drifting from his, glazed with boredom.

Because she can. Because I fulfilled a need until she found something better. Because acquisitions run her life. That's how things work in this world. Everything has a purpose. And when that's done, we move on. We consume anew. We never look back.

There had to be more than that.

He had to believe that there was more to his life than that.

So Theron took his inheritance, and left everyone behind.

Keeping to ground transportation, he travelled through cities and towns and plains, looking for the right amount of distance from Lea and the southeastern coast. Finally, in the North, as far north as he could go on the continent of Osha, he bought a house in Karum that was built into the edge of a cliff. He liked the security of the thick dirt walls, enclosing him on three sides. On the fourth side, he installed floor-to-ceiling windows, so he could always see who might be approaching; he couldn't quite quit the instinct to be watchful.

Of course, the Savas knew where he was, of course they did. Still, no one came after him, not enemy nor friend. Just as well.

Over the next eight years, he dabbled in different trades: engineering, computer hacking, business investments, martial arts. He took university classes remotely, under an assumed name, careful to minimize any personal interactions. He reduced his sleep to less than three hours per night. He meditated, and trained his body to be pliable and light, to feel nothing, to absorb nothing. Being alone became a natural state, and the idea of human touch became foreign, as did any desire for sex after a couple of professional encounters. It wasn't worth the hassle for temporary, reckless pleasure.

Instead, he began to make contacts, and take meetings with people across Osha: inventors, enforcers, fight promoters. For what purpose, he didn't quite know yet, but he had a burning need to find someone who could be loyal to him, and not to the Savas. He spent months looking at bodyguards and bounty hunters, retired law officers and mercenaries, looking for something to click. Nothing happened. No one had any semblance of something special until his meeting with a bounty boss in Queline, deep in the industrial North.

The boss himself was useless, Theron could tell within five minutes. Theron was on the brink of leaving when the door burst open. Three men dragged a woman inside, shoving her into a wooden chair, binding her arms behind her.

"Nicely done!" the boss crowed. "Did she give you much trouble?"

"Nah," one of the man scoffed. "Easy catch."

"Amazing bounty for this one," the boss told Theron. "Even better when they don't fight."

Curious, Theron eyed the woman in the chair. She was slumped over, her hair a hundred shades of blue: navy and aquamarine and sky-blue, jagged and flipping out at her shoulders. She wore gray athletic gear and heavy black boots. And her shoulders were rippling under the fabric.

She was breaking loose from her bonds, he realized.

Then her head lifted, and her eyes caught his: pale gray-green, framed with heavy black make-up, ghostly and piercing, furious and terrified.

There was the scraping sound of wood on wood.

The bounty hunters darted forward, and the world became a whirlwind of blood.

A gunshot rang out. The woman crashed to the floor, framed by the bodies of the three men.

The boss raised the barrel of his Aegis to fire a final shot into the woman's skull.

"Don't!" Theron burst out, surprising himself.

The Aegis swung in his direction.

Theron grabbed the man's arm, pushing the barrel away.

Somehow, the trigger was pulled.

Blood exploded all over Theron's chest and arms.

The boss crumbled, the Aegis clattering next to him.

When the roar died down in Theron's ears, the woman was the only other person breathing. But Theron couldn't move, couldn't blink. His thoughts berated him. *You can't be tied to this. You have to leave. Now. Now!*

She was taking in short, desperate gasps, curled into herself. The ground underneath her was soaked with blood. Theron heard his grandfather's voice in the back of his head: *Don't be stupid. Move your feet and keep walking. Who cares if she dies?*

No. No, he was better than that.

Hoisting her into his arms, her boots swinging over his elbow, Theron stepped over the still-warm bodies. His jacket grew warm and wet with her blood, then his dress shirt underneath. It struck him, as he stumbled down the stairs, that this was the first prolonged human touch he'd experienced in years. It was oddly intimate, cradling the woman against his chest, inhaling her foreign sweat, maneuvering through doors.

Within minutes, she was slumped in the passenger seat in the ground rover he'd rented, the doors locked and the windows drawn. He pressed one hand against the woman's side, thinking to staunch the flow of blood, but it just oozed between his fingers.

I need a medlab. And something discreet. Something charitable, somewhere far enough that she won't get tracked down.

A quick search of other industrial sites in the North. A brief longing look at the listing for Karum, so far away. Then Theron scanned the Midlands.

Yes, there, one small, almost imperceptible marker, deep within the plains, a Jala Communia. Jala was a religious faith, he remembered. Service to community. Charitable. They would help.

He set his destination, and set the rover on auto-drive. One hour. Could she survive that long? As the vessel sped over the pavement, then gravel, then grass, Theron riffled through the woman's pockets, searching for some kind of identification. A folded piece of paper was in one pocket: a professional fight listing for that date, with someone named Lora Blue with top billing.

Is this her? he wondered. He glanced at her face, half-hidden under the sprawl of blue hair. She was a mess, whoever she was. And she reeked of mekaline. Theron recognized the smell from his cousins.

Why was she worth so much money? Maybe the bounty was for unpaid drugs? He stuffed the flyer into his pocket and leaned back into his seat, trying not to react to her occasional twitches and moans.

Finally, a light broke through the black night, the silhouette of a gate, and a stone hut that glowed in the moonlight. He eased the rover behind the curve of a hill and cut the engines. Then Theron checked the pulse at the woman's throat. Still there, though the breath was strained.

Hoisting the woman in his arms again, Theron ignored the bald priest's threats, then pleas for him to leave, pushing his way into the clinic. It was small, and archaic, but it was the best he could do. He laid the woman on the gurney in the back of the clinic. Her eyes were rolled back into her head. She looked dead.

When he walked outside, the priest came after him, squawking with anger. Theron ignored him. Then the girl showed up. Sydel, looking like a ghostly child in her nightgown. Theron instructed her to get to work, and kept his pace.

He didn't stop moving until he was safely ensconced in his house in Karum. He shed the bloody clothes and burned them in the fire pit on the veranda.

Days later, the woman wandered back into his thoughts, with an unshakable curiosity. It didn't take long for Theron to

uncover information about Phaira Lora Byrne and her tumul-
tuous background: a mix of poverty, loss, and public disgrace.
He uncovered correspondence between a law enforcement officer, Aeden Nox, and one of Phaira's brothers, Renzo; they were
arranging the details of renting a Volante transport with the
intent of finding Phaira. She had disappeared from her hometown of Daro some weeks ago. He wondered if her brother was
still looking for her. Maybe she was on that Volante now.

When one of his algorithms caught that Jala girl, Sydel,
rifling through public records at a Vendor Mill, he made first
contact with Phaira. Her voice was different from what he expected, full of anger and paranoia. Theron spent the whole call
pacing the length of his house, his arm wrapped around his
head, working to keep his voice cold, perplexed as to why he
was even compelled to warn her about the breach in security,
and even more baffled why he suddenly insisted that Phaira
meet him in Daro so he could 'explain himself.'

This time, her eyes were clear: a ghostly gray-green against
the blue hair. She wore nanotube armor, her back straight as a
soldier's. Her arm muscles were pronounced, her aim unwaver-
ing when she pointed a military-grade Calis pistol at him. He
could see how she would succeed in the underground fighting
circuit, why she drew attention to herself. She refused to believe his story that he was just an innocent bystander when the
bounty hunters kidnapped her. But she never pulled the trigger.

Then a strange coincidence, weeks later; she was in Karum,
just minutes from his house of windows, alone, exhausted, and
looking for somewhere to hide. And when she came, he saw it

again when they sparred, when she met the challenges he tossed at her. Potential.

She might be an asset, he mused, *the partner I've been looking for.*

So, on a whim, he offered his house for her sanctuary. And to his surprise, she accepted.

For one week, their only contact was combat training sessions. She had trained in submissions, and he had focused on energetic redirection over the past eight years, so they both had techniques to teach. It was odd to be so physically close to someone, constantly on the verge of hurting each other, but at the same time learning every point of another's body. A strange, magnetic ripple grew in the basement, in those nights that they interacted. He couldn't tell if she felt something too. During the day, when she slept, he would roam the village, the beaches, anything to avoid his confusing fixation with this ex-soldier. Who wasn't exactly pretty, but when they were in the same room, he couldn't stop looking at her. Who was cradling his head when he woke from a stress-induced seizure, like she cared about him. Who held no regard for her life when it came to the safety of her dysfunctional family, a kind of devotion he didn't understand but desperately wanted to.

Then Phaira crawled through his window in Liera. He'd followed her to the city, bringing her beloved Calis pistols, left in Honorwell after a police raid, and stayed in the same building, just a few floors higher, in a safe house. He couldn't quite bring himself to leave; he enjoyed the limbo too much, of being neither here nor there.

Then one night, she appeared in his window. And over seven nights, her cool body was his: her soft moans; the flushed base of her throat; her fingernails in his back; the tiny scars underneath all that dark makeup, how they caught the moonlight when his face was an inch from hers. How she fell asleep next to him on her stomach, her arms over her head, her blue hair a matted mess. As she breathed, he remained on his back and shut his eyes, and though he couldn't sleep, he remained still, taking in the sensation of someone's body so close to his.

Until dawn broke, and she escaped back to her life, floors below. But something had broken open in him, some kind of unexpected, scorching desire, and like a fool, he waited for the night to come, his hands burning for her return.

To his surprise, in the silences between rushes, she started to talk to him. He learned about her parents, how she was an orphan like him, left to function alone from an early age. They both had troubled father figures, dysfunctional family relationships, and complicated romances that never lasted long. They both fought a persistent restlessness, and a swamping depression. They trusted very few people, having learned that most people were bound to disappoint. Her biggest fear was to make the wrong choice in who to trust, that her mistake would expose her as weak and vulnerable and ashamed. How nervous she was in those moments; how nervous they both were, underneath all the bravado.

But, too quickly, it was over,. He went back to Lea, and she went to the mountains in search of her family. But those nights in Liera resonated, like a film reel rolling in the back of his mind, brought into light when he closed his eyes, when he was smacked by his grandfather's cane and forced to perform menial housework as punishment for defying the order to return home.

But just like everything else in his life, the dream was bound to end.

And it did, three months ago.

First, that unexpected call from that girl, Sydel, and members of the original NINE group: Cyrah CaLarca and Kuri Nimat. They were calling to make amends. Amends! Theron kept the video dark so they couldn't see his rage. CaLarca denied any involvement in his family's death twenty-five years ago, but still apologized for her involvement, which was curious; Kuri had no remorse. When it was done, in the darkness of his apartment, he turned over the facts again and again. Phaira had allowed CaLarca onto her family's airship, the Arazura. She'd housed the woman, healed her, included her in group decisions, knowing that CaLarca was part of the NINE. Why would she do that? How could she do that?

It made sense soon enough, when Theron followed her to Macni, or "the Mac" as it was better known, a sprawling city on the East coastline. He watched as she shook hands with Detective Daryn Ozias on the front steps of the local patrol station. Theron recognized the detective immediately; the woman had woven in and out of Sava business for years.

Phaira was an informant.

She was manipulating him, and he'd walked into it.

Of course, his mind lectured. *She's already in league with your worst offenders, why wouldn't she be aligned with patrol? This whole time, her goal was to expose you and your secrets, to take you down through covert affection. Any logical person would believe that.*

If he were a true Sava, Theron would have her killed for embarrassing him. He would have killed her brothers, too, and anyone else she loved.

Instead, he pushed it aside. He hadn't disclosed anything that would hurt him. It was a passing infatuation. A game to play with a girl who was willing. Not worth his time and attention.

Only at night did Phaira come into his mind, frustrating dreams where he searched for her, just missed her exit from the room. Sometimes it was worse when she actually appeared in the dream, because she was always untouchable, at the other end of a crowd, too many witnesses preventing him from taking hold of her, from kissing her, from throwing her out of the window.

He woke up sore and exhausted, uncertain of what was real and what was fantasy. He hated those dreams, but he was grateful at the same time.

Better that it all came out in dreams. Better that it was cleaned out at night so he could function during the day, without thought, without emotion, without anything to distract him from his purpose.

III.

After a long negotiation of territory in Lower Lea, Theron left Bianco to wrap up the meeting with handshakes and half-hugs; an amazing conclusion, after so many hours of men yelling insults and threats.

The bodyguard, Grey, went first, as per usual, into the parking garage. Following steps behind, Theron did his best not to sigh audibly. Instead, he flicked open his Lissome, and did a quick search to see if there were any hits on his algorithms. For weeks now, he'd kept track of several persons of interest, peering into their changes of location, their transactions, their public appearances.

Anandi Ajyo, one match in the public network.

Theron slowed his step, glanced up to ensure that Grey wasn't watching him, and scanned the contents. The new leader of the Hitodama, a hacktivist group in the North, had a warrant issued for her arrest. What was that now, the second? Third?

She's getting sloppy, Theron mused. *She knows better.*

Still, Anandi's influence might be an asset at some point. They had no quarrel with each other; they knew each other as children, and their families were affiliated, but nothing more. It would be smart to keep her favor. When he got back to the apartment, he would alter the details of her warrant, just the tiniest details so a match would be impossible...

The lights went out in the garage.

Theron froze, searching for the silhouette of his bodyguard. He heard loud mouth breathing, and the click of a firearm safety being released.

Theron ducked behind another transport, reaching under his jacket for the concealed Sentry firearm. As he drew it out, he felt the familiar vibration in the barrel; the Sentry's safety was off, the gold ring on his middle finger sending the signal to release.

There was a yelp, followed by a high-pitched shriek.

The sounds of something liquid, squelching. Shuddering breaths turned into gurgling. Theron held his breath, every muscle tensed to attack. But he couldn't see anything.

The pavement vibrated beneath him. There were no more sounds.

Theron felt for the Lissome in his back pocket. His hands shook just a little as he twisted the device to activate a tiny flashlight. He aimed his Sentry with a straight arm before him, the Lissome crossed under his wrist to shine a path, and searched.

Blood was running into one of the sewer grates.

And Grey was facedown, the top of his head shining with three fresh gashes.

"Theron!" Bianco's cry echoed through the garage.

Theron swiveled, swinging his Sentry along with his gaze. The garage was silent, and empty.

The overhead lights flickered on, but a reddish haze lingered at the edge of Theron's peripheral vision. He swiped at his face, wondering if he was bleeding. Nothing was there.

The red cleared, finally, and the florescent lights illuminated the bodyguard's body, sprawled on the ground, blood gathering like a puddle of oil.

Meaty hands clapped down on Theron's shoulders. "My boy," Bianco panted. "Back inside, now. Now!"

Theron let himself be pulled into a transport's darkness and cold, re-circulated air, even as he shut his eyes tight and opened them, again and again, trying to find that trace of red.

* * *

One hour later, Theron sat in his leather armchair in his apartment, legs splayed, as he tried to process what happened only sixty minutes ago. "Do you know who is behind this?"

From across the room, Bianco let out a short, barking cough. "No."

Theron caught sight of Bianco's silhouette within the doorframe of his apartment. "You must have some ideas."

"I have suspicions," Bianco said. "A direct threat to you calls for severe retaliation, and the breaking of blood bonds. Even to attack those who serve you, it is madness."

"Someone from the outside, then?"

"Don't trouble yourself with it," Bianco soothed. "We have many things to do tomorrow, and you need to focus on appearing strong."

"Grey was just butchered in front of me," Theron retorted. "I think I'm staying inside for a while.'"

"Of course not," Bianco objected. "What kind of message does that send? You must be a man, be the leader that your grandfather - "

"All I've done is 'send the right message,'" Theron interrupted, pushing up out of the chair and rising to his full height of six-foot-six. "If it hasn't been received yet, then maybe I'm not the one for this job."

Bianco's voice was sharp. "Your grandfather would be disappointed."

"Well, that was a common event," Theron said sourly.

"Your grandfather loved you very much."

Theron snorted, turning away. He pressed a hand to the window, noting the ghostly condensation that formed around his fingers.

The sound of Bianco's heavy gait drew closer. The man stopped six feet away, perpendicular to him. "Did you ever think of how devastated he was to lose his two children, how it was to be the sudden guardian to four orphaned children who never knew him?" Bianco said quietly. "Who were soft and weak and spoiled? Look at you now, what a man you have become, a better man than your cousins -"

His voice cracked, and Theron felt a twinge of guilt. Bianco loved Iyo, there was no denying that fact. Bianco was still in mourning. The facts floated through Theron's head. He let them pass as Bianco kept talking. "He experienced nothing but loss. But he remained loyal and true to those who stayed, including me. You didn't know who your grandfather was, who he truly was..."

Bianco trailed off.

Theron didn't react.

"A new man is on his way now," Bianco said with a sigh. "We have a lot to accomplish, my boy. Remain strong. We will resolve this misunderstanding, make no mistake. You'll see."

* * *

"Get this over with as soon as possible," Jetsun instructed as they entered the Lea patrol station. "Say nothing unless I give you permission."

"Not certain why we're complying in the first place," Theron shot back, noting how the crowd parted as they walked through the front lobby. Jetsun had appeared at his apartment that morning with an official summons for questioning of Grey's murder, issued by none other than Detective Daryn Ozias (again, worming into Sava business!).

"Better to keep them satisfied, at least on paper," Jetsun said. "If you come in, they can't accuse you of stifling the investigation. The last thing we need is more attention on you for something like this."

"Fine," Theron interrupted her. "But I'll see her alone."

"Don't be foolish."

He shot her a look, and she fell silent.

She knows her place, he mused. *I suppose I have to live up to mine.*

"I'm right outside," she finally said. "If you need me, I'm right outside."

An officer opened the door for him. Theron ignored the man's stare and ducked through the doorframe. Inside, the room was darker than he expected. Theron hesitated, flashing back to the parking garage; there were too many shadows, too many options for concealment...

"Mr. Sava." Already seated at a metal table, Detective Daryn Ozias gestured to the seat across from her. "Jetsun isn't joining us?"

Theron said nothing. He yanked the metal chair so it scraped loudly across the floor, and folded his body down onto it. When seated, he fixed his glare on Ozias.

"Thank you for coming in," Ozias began. "My sympathies for your recent loss. I'm sure it was a great shock to you and your family."

"Question, Detective," Theron interrupted, tilting his head back to look at the broken lights in the ceiling. "Shouldn't an interrogation room be bright? What is this?"

"This isn't an interrogation," Ozias corrected. "But yes, I'm sorry, there've been budget cutbacks - "

"Why are you apologizing?" Theron broke in again.

Ozias' expression didn't change. "Being polite, I suppose."

"Not necessary," Theron said. "You've got five minutes. What do you want?"

"Was Grey's assassination meant for you?"

There was no point in lying. "Very well could have been."

"I've followed your family's activities for years, you know."

"If you're so well-informed, why bother to bring me in?" Theron emphasized the word *informed* with a rush of anger before he could reel it back. Ozias caught it, though. Theron saw the smallest shift in the woman's eye.

"Thought it would be good to meet the new heir to the throne, so to speak," Ozias said. "Especially when, upon succession, his bodyguard is killed in front of him. Maybe he's interested in talking. How much are you like your grandfather, I wonder?"

Is this your plan? Theron thought. *Trying to get me to brag, to declare my dominance over everything? Make denials and threats?*

At Theron's silence, Ozias activated the room's Lissome, projecting an info screen between them: a portrait of Grey, his body framed by the metal of the morgue. The deep gouges in his head, chest and throat had been closed to thin red lines. The pixels shuddered over the table.

"You want to tell me what happened that night?" the detective queried.

"I was walking to my town car," Theron said. "Grey went ahead of me, as always. Then the whole place went dark, I heard a noise, and he was dead when the lights came back up."

Theron saw the slightest twist in the woman's jaw. "And nothing else?"

"Were you really expecting details, Detective? Even if I had them, you wouldn't hear about it."

With a flick of her fingers, Ozias expanded the Lissome screen, so the camera zoomed to the gash at Grey's throat. Theron could see the ragged edges stitched together, the discoloration under the harsh fluorescent light. Theron's stomach turned, just a little. He didn't care much about the bodyguard, but it seemed like an awful way to die.

"The fatal wound to the throat wasn't administered with a knife," Ozias confirmed. "Nor any kind of clean blade. But metal, that we know. And tapered." She glanced at Theron. "Pretty unusual, even in your world."

"And why tell me these details?"

"I'm following protocol, Mr. Sava."

Theron looked at the image again. The detective was right. Business in the Sava family was resolved with a single gunshot, or a wire cord around the neck. Not with ripped flesh and bleeding out in public. So what was it, then? And was Grey the target? Or was Theron?

"I don't know what to tell you," Theron finally said. "I don't know what happened. But you've followed my family for long enough to know that it's time to step aside and let us deal with it."

Ozias jabbed a finger into the table. "This is a man's death. It might not mean much to you, given your family, but it deserves respect. And if there's a public threat, we need to address it. This goes beyond your borders, Mr. Sava."

Theron did the most infuriating thing he could think of: he shrugged one shoulder at the detective.

A knock at the door. Ozias shut down the Lissome, the digital screens sucked back into the square. The room went dark again.

"Stay in town," she warned Theron. "I might call you again."

"I'll decide whether or not to answer," Theron retorted. "If you keep clear of our affairs. And stop others from making that mistake."

Ozias frowned. "Who are you talking about?"

But Theron was already up and outside, Jetsun hissing at his side. "That was short. What did she say? What do I have to do?"

"Nothing," Theron said, quickening his stride. "It has nothing to do with you."

IV

Over the next week, the fervor around Grey's death began to lessen. Familiarity resumed: windows and wheels, marble and quartz, leather and mahogany. Another bodyguard arrived. Wicks was bigger, stronger, and heavily armed under the white suit that all protectors wore in the syndicate. Wicks trailed Theron on another date with a pre-selected girl. Time passed in a perfumed blur. Bianco seemed satisfied, hustling Theron from place to place, making introductions, watching from a distance. Only Jetsun seemed different: a little quieter, her amber eyes running over Theron at their weekly meeting, but quickly averted when he demanded she speak up.

He only had moments to check on his algorithms, in between supervision. The sudden death of entertainer Em Lee was still in the news, though the fervor had gone down over the weeks. The public was told that Em Lee died in a tragic mountain climbing accident, in the midst of a meditative retreat to prepare for her next album release. No news source identified Em Lee, real name Marette Lyung, as part of the original NINE. Nor did anyone seem to know that she was actually killed in Toomba after a shootout with the mountain militia, her body likely disposed in the caverns. It would probably never be public knowledge. But the sooner her name faded into memory, the better.

No correspondence from Renzo Byrne, or anyone else from that family, either.

Wicks remained by Theron's side as they entered his apartment building, and travelled in silence up the elevator. Even when Theron came to his door, Wicks remained six feet behind him.

"I'm fine," Theron instructed, a warning in his voice.

"I'm supposed to come in with you, sir," Wicks huffed. "Mr. Bianco isn't here, so he asked me to do a sweep."

"Not necessary." The last thing that Theron needed was this man peering into all his corners. It was bad enough that Bianco was always watching.

"I insist, sir."

"And I've given my order," Theron said icily. "Stay where you are."

The man nodded, straightening. "Yes, sir."

Locking the door behind him, Theron groped for the light sensor with the other hand, already exasperated with the effort, and the swallowing darkness.

Nothing happened.

He waved his hand again. Not even a spark.

His heart quickened, his eyes scanning for any sign of movement. There was none. But the walls of his living room looked strange.

He crept closer, trying to make out the detail.

There was a jagged, horizontal path running across the middle, around the whole perimeter of the living room, the drywall ragged as ripped skin.

Then the edges turned a strange shade of red.

And on the other side of the front door, there was a heavy thump.

* * *

A clean-up crew and a bottle of liquor later, Theron was somewhere between dreams and hallucinations when he heard the sound of his name. Slumped in the chair behind his desk, he squinted across his apartment, trying to determine if the dark silhouette on his threshold was real.

"Mr. Sava, can you hear me?"

Theron forced his eyes to focus. It was Detective Ozias. Startled, Theron rubbed his palm over his face, sniffing in a deep breath. "Sorry," he said automatically, before chiding himself.

Ozias smiled at him, though it was more like a wince. "Do you need something? Some water, perhaps?"

"No," Theron said. "You shouldn't be here."

"A little hard to stay away, Mr. Sava." The detective glanced over her shoulder. "So what happened this time?"

What could Theron say, really? He had left Wicks to his death. Someone had scratched a horizontal path through the walls of his apartment, then did the same to Wicks, ripping him in half. Maybe if he'd let the bodyguard come in, the man would still be alive. His gaze wandered to the faint remnants of blood splatter on the walls in the hall. The crew had missed a few spots here and there. And on the ceiling too. Arterial spray was a killer.

"Take my advice, Detective," Theron finally said. "It's not necessary." How many times could he warn the woman to back off? People would get to know her face, her nosiness, if they didn't already, and one wrong word, one perceived insult....

From far away, the clunk of elevator doors. Then Bianco appeared, a murderous look on his face. "Out," he spat at the detective. "Now. This is private property."

"This is a homicide," Ozias said. "And potentially a serial killer."

Shut up, Detective, Theron thought. *Shut up if you know what's good for you.*

Bianco shook his head again and again, so infuriated that he didn't seem able to speak. "Out, now!" he finally barked. "No more talk, no more questions!"

Her hands lifted, Ozias slid past the furious Bianco and disappeared.

Bianco took out a handkerchief, mopping his brow. Then he threw it to the ground with a sudden grunt, strode across the room, and shoved Theron in the chest.

"What are you doing?" Theron exclaimed.

But Bianco lifted a finger to his face. "You tell me the truth now. Did they anger you?"

"What?"

Bianco's voice grew whispery and sympathetic. "Is this some kind of revenge? Because you have been put in this position? Understand now, you don't know the harm you are doing, in acting this way."

"I didn't kill them!" Theron said, taken aback. "Is that what you think happened? That I lost control and killed them?"

"I promise, Theron," Bianco soothed. "I would not judge you if you did. Your grandfather had his moments, too. But we are in a delicate state, until your position is official...."

Bianco trailed off, patting Theron on the arm.

The silence stretched on and on. The longer it went, the more Theron questioned the red haze he'd seen both times, before the murders. Maybe his personality was split in two, after so many seizures. Maybe he should have listened of that doctor, had new brain scans done....

"You make a statement," he heard Bianco murmur. "You show them that you are taking this seriously. Start with the likely suspects. And I will stay with you, Theron, and protect you myself. You have my word."

* * *

Bianco was always with Theron now, even sleeping over, the sounds of his snoring coming through the walls. Tripwires were installed around the apartment. An armored car was ordered. Meetings were set up to interrogate various syndicate connections. Muscle would have to be thrown around, if it were to be seen as effective. It wasn't Theron's style, but there were rules to follow. There was no time alone to work on his plans; Bianco was always there, peering over his shoulder, ordering around the staff that now flitted nervously from room to room, patching over the horizontal rip in the wall, scrubbing every stain and smell from the hallway. Theron felt like a petulant child. Someone might as well just lift him by the arms and carry him to and fro, like a toddler. Even in his own bedroom, he felt eyes and ears just beyond the wall. It was too risky to do anything but lie in bed and try to figure out how to get rid of all these people. What if he took one of Bianco's women as a lover? He had to gain privacy from that move. Then, when the doors were locked, he could pay for the girl's silence, for her to go into another room and close the door. Make it a business arrangement.

And if she talked, regardless? And if she spied?

There was no way.

Theron spent long hours in the dark wondering if he should just give up and accept his role. There was a neat path to follow to make everyone happy, with all the advantages of luxury, splendor and stimulation. Why not just take it? It would be easy. True, something inside of him would shrivel up and die, but at least he would be comfortable. He could have a wife, children, grandchildren. He could do all the things that men were supposed to do.

Maybe they would bring him joy in the end.

* * *

Jetsun's law firm buzzed with activity: digital images from Lissomes hovering over cubicles, hushed voices making threats. But, as usual, everything slowed down, and everyone quieted as Theron headed for his cousin's corner office. Every eye was fixed on him, some directly, most keeping him in their peripheral vision as they pretended to adjust their lapels or flip a page. He was tempted to do something unexpected. Yell at the top of his lungs, do a cartwheel, even smile and say good morning. It would all have the same effect: surprise and fear. The only option was to keep his stride, and enjoy being unaccompanied for once. Bianco let him be whenever he went to his cousin's office, and the bodyguards stayed by the elevator.

As he approached, Jetsun appeared, her tight smile greeting him. He braced himself for the familiar lecture: that he should just focus on the matters at hand, leave the NINE business for another time, it would still be there in a year when things had settled and everything was in proper control, especially with this new threat looming over them. He had the feeling, though, that if he abandoned this routine, if he didn't take at least one small step forward, any hope he still held onto would be swept away and lost forever.

For once, though, Jetsun didn't hiss at him on his approach, or make some kind of sly joke. Instead, her smile remained tight, and her eyes swept the space behind him.

"What is it?" he asked.

"Come in," she told him. "I'll be back in ten minutes."

As he entered her lush office, a second blond head swiveled. For once, Theron was thoroughly shocked. "Renzo."

"Hey," Renzo Byrne nodded at him.

As the door closed behind them, a flurry of emotions sparked in Theron's brain: anger, confusion, suspicion. He cleared his throat. "Are we - are we here to make a deal?"

Renzo said nothing. The man's gaze had a wary intensity that made Theron uncomfortable. "Well?" he prodded.

"You all right?" was Renzo's response. "I heard about what's been going on."

Theron bristled. "From who?"

"Rumors. I almost cancelled, but Jetsun assured me it was safe."

"Of course it's safe," Theron said. "It's part of the business. Now why are you here?" A thought struck him. "Are you alone?"

"Just me today," Renzo said. "CaLarca's back on the *Arazura*."

The sound of Cyrah CaLarca's name made Theron want to throw a chair across the room. That NINE woman was still there, under their protection? Theron burned for specifics. But he couldn't. Time was limited. The blinds were drawn, but anyone could walk in looking for Jetsun, and cause trouble. He had to temper down his anger and remain cold.

Renzo shrugged and crossed his arms. "So you're looking to mass-produce HALOS. What do you need from me? A signature?"

Theron blinked. "Yes, that, and I'll buy you out at whatever price you name."

Renzo shrugged again. "You helped me with the *Arazura*, and so many other things. So take the HALO design. Take sole ownership. I won't contest."

Was this some kind of negotiation? "You don't mean that," Theron challenged.

"I have enough to deal with." The man's gaze remained steady, and piercing. "Besides, I'm not so sure where your rana comes from these days, and if I'd keep it in the end. No offense," he added.

Yes, the man had a point. There was always the possibility of scrutiny, with Theron's name attached; additional paperwork, government take-back. Would Renzo want to get entangled? Of course not.

Theron had the sudden impulse to be honest with this man, with someone for once. "The HALOS will be legitimate," he told him. "Separate from everything else, even from the Sava accounts. It'll do good things against -"

He didn't say the word NINE out loud, but Renzo nodded just the same.

Theron smirked. They were a lot alike.

"You know, Renzo," he added with a rush, "if things were different, and if I thought you'd agree, I'd ask you to be my partner in the business. See what else we could come up with, you know?"

Renzo's mouth quirked in a half-smile. "That'd be something."

Then something shifted in his face. "You really don't look so good. I mean, can I - can we do something, or - ?"

"Thanks," Theron told him, grateful for the attention, but still firm. "You should go."

"Take care of yourself, man."

And with that, the man was gone.

Two minutes later, Jetsun's blonde head peered around the doorframe. "I took him out the back way," she confirmed. "Are we done? Did you make an agreement?"

"He made a proposal," Theron said. "But I think I'm going to refuse."

"What? Why?"

Because it's not right. I'm furious with him, with all of them, but it's not right. There has to be a better way to go about this, a fairer way, a more collaborative way....

He couldn't say any of that out loud, of course.

"I've made the connection. Let it be," he told his cousin. "Then I'll counteroffer."

V.

The newest bodyguard, Kurtz, shuttled Theron through the rain, doing his best to hold the black umbrella over his head, but instead bumping him and blocking his vision. Annoyed, Theron swiped the umbrella from the man's wet palm, and strained to see through the downpour, into the night, where only a few streetlights flickered. The meeting with Upper and Lower Lea bosses had ended with a cautious note. Nothing was said about the dead bodyguards. There were even a few nods of approval, some second looks, sizing him up. Perhaps they were finally beginning to trust him.

Kurtz had been offered up by one of the syndicate families in Upper Lea. Kurtz was huge, silent, and had a snake-like quality about him. When anyone even jostled Theron, Kurtz was there, shoving them back. Some noses were broken. Bianco loved him. Theron was already exasperated.

Kurtz popped open the passenger door, and Theron slid inside, brushing the water off his suit jacket. Soon, the transport began to crawl down the street. Theron stared at the gutters through the window. Flash flooding might be a problem; he could see streams rushing into the sewers.

There was a dull thud, and the transport lurched. Theron pounded on the driver's partition window. "Why are you stopping?" he yelled.

"I hit something," Kurtz shouted back. "I gotta get it out of the way."

The bodyguard opened the driver's side door and slid out into the darkness. The rain pounded on the car roof. The moist scent of the city wafted in, garbage and smoke. Theron took in breaths through his mouth, already sullen at the thought of replacing the man. If Kurtz hit someone with the transport, he was already drawing too much attention.

A minute passed. Theron craned his neck, opening the window, trying to see. "Kurtz!" he hollered. "Back here, now!"

There was no response. Looking over the divider, through the car windshield, Theron followed the trail of the headlights, breaking through the drops like a hazy moonlit path. Nothing but gray and concrete. The constant pounding of rain on metal made him disoriented.

A shimmer of movement outside.

Theron leaned forward, squinting.

Then he recoiled as the silhouette came into view, scrambling backwards until his back pressed against the opposite door.

In the sparse light, Theron saw that the person was shrouded and hooded in folds of red cloth, its face covered with a metal mask, carved with sharp, ugly features. The person lifted a hand, and drew on the passenger window with the edge of its index finger.

The slow, sickening shape of a heart, drawn in red.

In blood, Theron realized.

Then, just as quickly as it appeared, the creature was gone.

* * *

One of the minor families shuttled Theron to Jetsun's brownstone building, and his cousin was there at the door to usher him inside.

"Are you sure you want me in here?" Theron deadpanned, sauntering through the foyer. "I'm not having the best fortune with those in my circle."

"Stop it."

Theron glanced at his cousin. Were there tears in her eyes? Theron had never seen her cry before. Over Kurtz, really? Or was it more about the fear?

"Theron," Jetsun told him. "You need to bring in Phaira Lore."

Cold splashed over him, as if doused in ice water. He refused to let anything show, though. "For what?" he asked lightly. "I've had plenty of company lately."

"For protection, of course."

"Don't be ridiculous."

"Why is that ridiculous?"

"Because this is a private matter." He emphasized the last words, as if speaking to a child.

"You don't have the choice anymore," Jetsun shot back.

"I always have the choice." He said the sentence with a warning.

"When this gets out, everyone is going to panic," she hissed. "They already fear that you're losing your mind -"

Then her voice caught. "You'll kill us all if you don't do something."

Coward. Jetsun's words came back to haunt him. *Wimp. Unable to speak up. Unable to do anything right.*

"Not an option," he snapped.

"You're not thinking straight."

"Don't insult me," Theron shot back, a dangerous anger coiling inside him.

But Jetsun continued to push: "You don't need more dumb muscle. You need someone who is smart. Who can outwit whoever is doing this."

Annoyed, Theron went for the door. Jetsun blocked him. "Which is why you will put your little crush aside, and recruit any and all resources available," she told him pointedly.

"I'm not 'recruiting' anyone," Theron snapped. "Got it?"

He yanked open the door. For a moment, he expected a shotgun blast to rip through his chest; that everything so far had been a lead-up to this great, dramatic ending. But there was nothing but the minor family outside, peering up at him. He scowled at them. They averted their eyes.

"She owes you," Jetsun said under her breath, from behind. "They all owe you."

The notion of payback was a common one in Theron's world. It colored almost every transaction, who owed what, who still had debt to resolve. Objectively, Jetsun was correct; the Byrne family did owe him an enormous debt. He was the one who disabled the bounty on Phaira. He paid off the officers in Honorwell to forget about Phaira and her mad escape with Anandi and Emir Ajyo. And her younger brother Cohen would have been lost or killed had he not interferred.

But even with all those facts, this was different. He'd done all those interventions for purely selfish reasons: to appease his foolish infatuation with Phaira. And even though he was bitter now, he still respected her brothers.

"The answer is no," Theron said over his shoulder. "To all of it."

* * *

When Theron told him of his decision, Bianco didn't seem to register the words. So Theron repeated himself, speaking slowly and forcefully, as if to push the words into the old man's brain and make him understand.

When Bianco finally spoke, it was a statement: "You cannot be alone."

"Whoever is behind this," Theron said. "He isn't touching me. Only those around me. So I'm going to eliminate the targets and see what happens."

"I can't allow that, son."

"I'm not your son, and it's not your choice," Theron reminded him. "I'll conduct my business from here on out. No one is to stand guard, or initiate contact with me." As he said the words, a little thrill went through him. Finally alone, finally able to concentrate on his plans.

"As your appointed advisor - "

"That appointment is over," Theron said.

Bianco's eyes bulged. "Are you firing me?"

"Not at all," Theron said. "I'm releasing you from your bonds. Go be with your family."

"You are my family," Bianco said gruffly. "You, your cousins, your grandfather."

The sentiment made Theron uncomfortable. He didn't see it like that at all. Bianco was his grandfather's friend and right-hand man, of course, but he had nothing to do with Theron and his cousins growing up. Maybe it was age that was making the man emotional, trying to forge a bond wherever possible. It just irritated Theron, the delay, the arguing.

"I have travelled for miles on your behalf," Bianco continued, a strangled edge to his words. "Across lines, making peace, gathering supporters. Many of whom required a great deal of convincing. Without me, they will splinter."

They would. That was true. Perhaps he was being too rash. Bianco was necessary.

No. He wanted nothing more than to be away from Bianco's sticky fingers and posturing. And he couldn't be bothered to make any more excuses. The old man should feel lucky that Theron was working to spare his life and keep him far from the danger.

"I won't repeat myself," he told his former advisor. "Go. And tell everyone to stay away."

* * *

But, within the day, Jetsun sent Theron messages, asking if he knew where Bianco was.

Theron remained silent, working feverishly in his apartment, curtains closed, windows shut, papers and Lissomes around him.

Her warnings grew more and more frantic. "Something is very wrong," she insisted. "Why aren't you responding to me? Stop ignoring me and say something!"

He did nothing, though a tiny stone settled in his stomach, one that wouldn't quite lift.

Instead, a hundred times that day, Theron thought about dying. Of just giving up his plans, opening the door, and welcoming the assassin inside to slit his throat. It was coming, wasn't it? This was all some kind of sick set-up, with Theron as the final target. Enough of surrounding himself with human shields. It would be a relief, in so many ways, if everything was to end.

But nothing happened. Night stretched into dawn, and noon until sunset, and no one came, no one broke in. No shadows crossed the windows.

Then Jetsun called him again the next morning, her voice thick with tears.

Bianco's body had been found.

Dental records identified him publically, though the gold ring on his charred finger marked his true position. An accelerant had been poured on him, and set on fire. A slow, agonizing, screaming death.

The only piece of evidence was a heart scratched in the pavement next to the body.

* * *

Funeral arrangements were swift. The morning of the service, Theron bathed, put on a fresh suit, and attended. Every parishioner gave him a wide berth. He heard curses muttered, saw bright-red faces. Someone might have spat on the ground, but his eyes were so blurry that he couldn't be certain. Instead, he stood by, and let Jetsun give the orders. Her face was veiled, but he could see the Lissome piece affixed at her jawline, heard the slow hush of her voice, giving orders.

Then Theron returned to his apartment in Lea, out of routine more than anything else. Not that he wanted to be there, but there was nowhere else to go, and it didn't much matter if there were. If the assassin didn't kill him, the rest of the Syndicate would, now that Bianco was dead. The fourth death in proximity to Theron. It was all over.

No one knocked on his door in the days that followed, not even Jetsun. Theron slept on his white chesterfield for thirty minutes at a time, his dreams growing more violent. Even worse, they lingered. He was having trouble sorting out his memories, what was real, and what was created. Every person in his head seemed to swirl together, taunting him, mocking him. He obsessed over those hearts left behind, one in blood, one in stone. Meant for him, but why? What did it symbolize?

And why hadn't that red assassin come for him yet? They had already proven that it could reach Theron wherever he was, no matter who he surrounded himself with. Whoever this person was, they were destroying his reputation, turning the world against him, but leaving him alive. Why? Were there more targets?

Jetsun, he thought immediately. *She is in the crosshairs, she has to be. Who else is left?*

On the other hand, everyone in Lea adored Jetsun Sava. She was a far more public figure than he or Bianco; a philanthropic leader in Lea, well-known by every resident. There was even a charity event planned for that night, he remembered, in spite of everything that had happened.

She is a shield, he thought. *If she is hurt or killed, there will be an uproar. Media attention will come with it. This person might not want that. They want to hurt me, not become a target.*

The buzz of the doorbell jolted him from his thoughts. His face was itchy; he rubbed his palm over the growth on his jaw, noting how his long black hair had come loose.

The doorbell buzzed again. Whoever rang his doorbell? Usually it was a pounding at the door, or his Lissome vibrating on the table with impatience.

He forced himself to his feet. His impulse was to grab a weapon. But he didn't care.

To the right of the doorframe, an info-screen flickered into view, displaying the faces of those waiting on his doorstep.

His heart almost jolted out of his chest.

PART TWO

I

In the darkness of her hostel room, Phaira admitted the truth. She missed her brothers. She missed Sydel, and Anandi and Emir. She even missed CaLarca a little. And deep down, she was lonely for Theron Sava. Not just physically, though the yearning was so bad sometimes she thought she might crack open. No, it was more than that, and on the nights when her feelings broke through, she drank them away, trapping herself in the moment until everything went black. It was all too difficult at night, when everything was quiet, and every thought came to a head.

In the daylight, she had a purpose. She'd been travelling for weeks now, trekking through towns and countryside to uncover whatever she could about the NINE, stopping only for a quick meal, a pair of replacement boots, some shelter to catch some sleep, before moving on. Detective Daryn Ozias, her secret sponsor, wired a fresh stack of rana every week, along with any updates, records on persons of interest, suggestions for her next destination. But the travel allowance wasn't much, and it was meant to stretch, so Phaira stuck with the cheapest, slowest forms of travel, all the way across the Midland prairies and into the South. It meant wearing the same clothes for days on end, wringing them in a sink and sleeping naked under worn sheets. It meant the cheapest way to get drunk on the nights she needed a release: liquor poured from cobwebbed bottles that broke when pulled away from the bar, its syrup caked in a raw circle on the shelf.

And really, Phaira didn't care about the conditions. She was used to living on scraps. There was only so much that she really needed. And being so tight with rana meant that she didn't have enough to buy mekaline, in those moments when she was so tired and muddled that she would have traded a week's meals for one hit of the drug.

After she'd made the agreement with Ozias, set up an account for deposits, and received the temporary patrol badge that would protect her on the road, Phaira's first stop was the Jala Communia, Sydel's former commune, nestled deep in the Midlands. Phaira had been there twice before, first as a patient, second as a reluctant resident, trying to tease out NINE knowledge from the commune's master, Yann Qin.

This third time, she came in sympathy for their recent loss.

Inside the latticework gates, the commune looked the same: orange-pink stone walls, evergreens and farm fields, neat barracks, white stone medical clinic on the outskirts. Inside, everyone had the same dazed expression on their faces, their movements slow, as if through water.

Weeks ago, Yann had suffered a heart attack. Kuri Nimat had only arrived an hour prior, demanding entry, and the two men were in deep, private conversation in Yann's cell when Kuri came running out of the barracks, yelling for help. Kuri even tried to revive him, the new Jala medic said soberly, but it was too late.

"Was it a natural death?" Phaira pressed. She didn't fully understand the NINE, but she felt certain that Kuri could have stopped Yann's heart out of spite.

The medic frowned. "There's nothing to suggest otherwise."

"I know what Yann was capable of," Phaira warned him. "If there's any suspicion, anything at all, tell me."

The man faltered. "I don't know what you mean. What are you suggesting?"

Phaira eyed the man hard, wondering if he was a smooth liar. But she couldn't tell. Was she losing her edge?

Yann Qin was buried in the plains, just outside Jala's walls. There was a stone marker in the dip of a valley, the mound of unturned dirt starting to grow grass again. Phaira stood over Yann's gravesite. Satisfaction simmered next to any hint of sympathy she had for the man. He had never been kind to her, and, by his admission, he mind-wiped Sydel so many times that the girl's brain was permanently damaged. And Yann was one of the original NINE, too. Better that he was gone. It was easier to think that, to scratch out his name, and move on.

The second destination took her southwest, to the base of the Cyan Mountains, to Zangari's public gardens, where the entertainer Em Lee held her last public concert. Memorials spilled over the grounds, flowers and signs and blown-up photographs of the blonde dreadlocked superstar. Phaira had only seen the woman behind the Em Lee persona once: Marette Lyung, another NINE member, who was shot dead in Toomba. Funny how the community was still in mourning; even weeks later, the story of Em Lee's tragic death from mountain climbing remained a headline. She wasn't that much of a celebrity, at least from what Phaira could see, and she hadn't added much to the world in her lifetime.

It took some time to track down Em Lee's former security guards and concert technicians. But they all cited their confidentiality contracts as an excuse to remain silent, shaking their head at the fact that their former employer was dead and the contract was invalid, no matter what she threatened.

She was definitely losing her edge.

Phaira's next task was to investigate the Joran Asanto Foundation and estate. It wasn't on the list, exactly, and Ozias questioned her judgment in asking to do it in the first place, but it was for Sydel, the long-lost Asanto daughter, as she had only recently learned.

Learning about the Asanto estate was not as difficult as she feared; Joran Asanto's rana went far, even twenty years after his death. An anonymous beneficiary was in charge of the Foundation, which retained a stellar reputation over the past two decades: low overhead, high level of charitable contributions to the public, everything that was supposed to be. Yet there was something about it that made Phaira itch. Maybe because she knew the rightful heir to all that rana, and who should really be controlling its flow. Sydel had never known her parents, Joran and Tehmi Shovann, as they'd died when she was only days old, but their estate was hers, legally, should she want to take it. Whether that would ever happen, Phaira couldn't imagine. But she could give the girl the information, and let Sydel decide her fate.

Now Phaira was in the South, as far south as she'd ever been. Her destination: CaLarca's old farm. She studied the satellite map on her Lissome, dreading what she might find.

She could smell smoke from a kilometer away; the stench was soaked into the greenery. There were no sounds of wild-life as Phaira followed the dirt road, shaded by the overhang of great, looming trees. Then the site of the fire was before her: remnants of the farmhouse, piles of black rubble, glimmers of metal. She knelt down with a branch and sifted through the rubble, looking for clues, wondering if she might come across bones. There were supposed to be two people living here. CaLarca's partner, Ganasan, was one of the original NINE, and designated as an Insynn, with precognitive abilities. They had a son, Bennet, two years old.

"He wouldn't leave our home," CaLarca insisted when Phaira pressed. "No matter the threat."

If that's true, Phaira mused, turning over a blackened chunk of wall, *then he's dead.*

But as she continued to search, there was no sign of hu-man remains in the wreckage, just hints of a life: half-melted silverware; a charred stuffed animal, broken dishes scattered. CaLarca's life,

A shimmer caught Phaira's eye, under the white ash. She blew carefully, sending granules in the wind, clearing without touching.

There sat a bead, one-half inch in diameter, blue, and un-damaged. When she put on her reading glasses and peered into its center, Phaira could make out a swirl, like some pale hurri-cane in the middle. Was this CaLarca's? Or Ganasan's? No sign of any other beads or stones in the pile, no hole in the bead to indicate it was part of a necklace or bracelet.

It might be valuable. She could find a neutral eye in town to tell her what it was, and how much it was worth. Maybe she was just being paranoid when it came to CaLarca. The green-haired woman owed them all so much. This would serve as partial debt paid.

Phaira stood, pocketing the bead and wiping her hands on her pants. Then she searched the landscape for paths into the woods, tire marks, anything that might suggest that Ganasan and Bennet escaped the fire. They couldn't have just been lifted into the air – could they? Could they levitate? She didn't know what to think of what the NINE might be capable of.

Click. The unmistakable sound of a rifle being primed.

Her hand skirted to her thigh, where her Calis handgun would typically be holstered. If Anandi had ever given them back after Honorwell, she lamented, and wondered if she should go for the knife concealed in her boot.

She looked over her shoulder. Fifty feet away, at the property border, there was the shape of a farmer, grizzled and wrinkled, his rifle cocked against his shoulder.

"Stay there," he ordered. He had the same accent as CaLarca, soft consonants.

He was alone. No signs of any backup. Just a scared local. It would be a risk, but the man's hand was steady, and the buckshot would be devastating.

So she lifted her hands in the air. "I'm with patrol," Phaira called out. "Not looking to make any trouble. Just investigating.

"You're either a liar, or a terrible investigator," the farmer called back. "The fire happened weeks ago."

"It took some time to get this far south," Phaira said. "I'm here on behalf of Cyrah CaLarca."

The barrel of his rifle lowered just a little.

"You their neighbor?" Phaira tried.

"Might be." The rifle steadied. "But there's been enough strangers wandering around, destroying things. Don't think you can touch my farm and burn it to the ground, too."

"Not interested in your farm," Phaira said carefully. "Only this one. Did you see who set the fire?"

"No. And I told the real patrol that."

Phaira ignored the dig. "I'm just trying to help a - a friend."

"She was a strange one. CaLarca.

"Yeah, I've learned that," Phaira agreed.

"Ganasan was a good man, though. Good neighbor. Quiet, kept to themselves mostly. Their little boy was cute, too. They didn't deserve this. No one does." The man paused, thinking. "She's alive?"

"Yes," Phaira said. "Do you think Ganasan and Bennet are?"

"Can't say," the man said. "Didn't see anyone coming or going. Just the fire in the night."

Phaira withdrew the bead from her pocket, holding it between thumb and forefinger. "Have you seen this before? I found it in the ash, but it's not attached to anything."

The man squinted, and shook his head.

Disappointed, Phaira pocketed the bead again, scanning the landscape again. Ozias wouldn't be pleased to know that the rana spent to travel this far south had uncovered no new information.

"Talk to my friend in town," the man interrupted her thoughts. "Maybe he sold it to them. He knows all the transactions in the area. I can give you a ride. Got a few stops to make first, but you can go in the back of the truck."

"If you're finished with your investigation," he added pointedly, the barrel of his rifle making a lazy circle in the air.

II

Phaira spent the next hour surrounded by crates full of vegetables, and swinging security straps that the farmer didn't seem to see the point of using. Trying to will off a growing headache, to distract herself, Phaira cupped the blue bead in her hand, enjoying the cool pressure against her palm. With her other hand, she activated her Lissome and sent messages: to Renzo, letting him know that she was on the road again; to Cohen, asking him to please get in touch with his older brother so he would stop worrying; to Ozias, informing the detective that her allowance for travel was almost gone.

Then she bit her lip, and punched in a new connection code, leaving only the audio intact.

"Phaira!"

"Hey, Sydel. You busy?

"No, having a rest, actually. We've been busy all day." There was satisfaction in the girl's voice, mixed with fatigue. Phaira recalled their last video conversation from a week ago. Sydel's copper hair was growing out again. Her braids hacked off in Toomba during her breakdown, Sydel's hair was smoother now, curling around her forehead and ears. She almost looked cute, and peaceful, a far cry from the scared, crumbling girl she was on the *Arazura*, not so long ago.

"Where are you now?" Phaira asked.

"Approaching Queline via train. Emir has some appoint-
ments set up. I'm in the back car, doing some homework he's
assigned. Reading up on infectious diseases."

"Be careful over in Queline," Phaira warned. "It's got some
bad areas. Keep away from the bridges, that's where all the drug
deals go down."

"Noted." There was a long pause. "How are you? Where are
you now?"

"Still south. Checking leads. Nothing much to report, not
yet, anyways."

"Well, something's on your mind. What is it?"

"What makes you think you know what's going on in my
head?"

"Because I do. What's the matter?"

Phaira's fingers hovered over her encrypted Lissome, wondering whether to make some excuse and disconnect the line.
These conversations felt almost like an invasion. Sydel was
building her own life as a medical professional. Maybe these
calls were an inconvenience. Maybe the girl was better off
without her influence.

"Come on, Phaira."

The girl's impatience made Phaira smile, despite herself.
"I've just had a lot of time on my own," she admitted. "Time
to think about things, and what I might want to do when I get
back home."

"Have you talked to Cohen lately?" she added, wondering if
it was the wrong thing to ask. She was nervous to ask her little
brother, who was so silent and brooding now, so unwilling to

share what exactly he was doing up there in Toomba, living with their grandmother, enmeshed in that mountain militia.

"A while ago." But Sydel went silent after that. So who knew if the two of them were speaking? Phaira hoped they were.

But the silence was growing awkward, and Phaira didn't have the nerve to ask, nor the energy to get into a bigger discussion. This was just a check-in call, nothing more. "I should go."

"As should I. I have a lot of preparations to make."

"I'm glad things are going well for you, Sydel."

"Be safe, Phaira. I hope you find what you are looking for."

When she disconnected, Phaira glanced out the cargo window. Outside, the world was awash in pink and gold.

Sydel's words lingered in her mind. *What I'm looking for. What I'm looking for.*

What was Phaira going to do when this was over? When this mission was finished, when the contract with Ozias was closed and her temporary badge returned? What then?

Her mind turned with possibilities as she watched the sun set.

She could ask for regular work detail from Detective Ozias. Maybe there were other areas that she could investigate independently, under the shadow of law patrol. Osha had a lot of dark corners, especially in the West, which Phaira was more and more curious to learn about, given her discoveries.

She could accompany Sydel and Emir on their travels, maybe help them navigate the rougher areas. She was useless as a medical aide, but maybe there was some use for her skills. She liked them both; they made her feel calmer, less anxious.

She could branch off on her own as a Locate-Retrieve-Protect specialist. After the Kings incident, 'Phaira Lore' had been exposed by an unknown source, who called her an LRP. Work might be available if she sought it out.

She could ask Theron Sava for a chance.

A chance at what, though?

Their interactions were nothing but sex and a few confessions. They had no basis in reality, and she preferred the dream.

Or so she thought, before she started travelling and seeking clues. Now she wasn't sure. She'd seen so much over the past few months, and again and again, her first thought was the desire to tell Theron Sava about it. She couldn't quite push aside that immediate reaction to know what he thought, to hear him sum up the truth of the conflict with a succinct comment, or those little truths that cut, for better or for worse.

Phaira stared at the edge of the sun until her eyes burned. Even if she were to take the leap, what did she want? To set up a regular time and place to sleep together? To establish some form of dating relationship? Every scenario made her cringe. Nothing made sense; nothing seemed to fit.

If it's so impossible, then why doesn't this ache go away?

She had no answer for that.

* * *

The jeweler's shop was dusty, cramped with the smells of different metal, and claustrophobic, with only one visible exit. Phaira remained still, however, and watchful, waiting for his verdict. In turn, his eye, magnified through the spyglass, often shifted to sweep over her again.

Finally he spoke: "Where did you get this?"

"I take it you've never seen it before? Or sold it to anyone nearby?"

"No." He peered through the lens. "The bead is solid glass, but the center is moving independently."

"It's moving?" How had Phaira missed that detail? Sure enough, when she borrowed the eyeglass, the faded swirls inside the bead were rotating counterclockwise, so slowly that it took a few seconds to recognize the movement.

"What is this?" she asked out loud. "How do you make something like that? Does it symbolize something?"

"You're not from here."

Phaira glanced up. The man's elbows squeaked against the glass. She could make out the long, curling hairs on his ears, like little wings brushed back.

Wary, she slid back her hood so he could see her face clearly, the blue hair at the edges. "I'm not from here," she confirmed.

"You here because of the Reed fire?"

Phaira thought about lying. "I'm looking for answers," she finally said. Then she eyed the jeweler. "You have anything to share?"

The jeweler nodded at the bead, now nestled in a patch of velvet. "That's not from here either. The outer shell was made with sand from the West."

Then the man held up his hands. "That's all I can tell you, though, without cracking it open and seeing what happens." His voice grew nervous. "At least you can tell that to your boss. Don't mention my name, though, please do me that favor. I don't want any trouble, or visitors wanting more 'details.' That's all I can offer. Please go now."

Boss? Visitors?

Phaira opened her mouth to question him further, but the man was already gone, politely ignoring her, as he helped another customer.

Exhaustion came over her like a wave. She was out of leads, almost out of rana, and her clothes were one wash away from falling apart. The bead was odd, but nothing to go on. She would give it to CaLarca as proof that she had gone to the farm.

It was time to go home.

III.

Phaira. Hey. Phair."
Someone was calling her name impatiently, and somewhere in the back of her mind, she heard the click of metal on
metal: her brother Renzo's prosthetic leg, shoeless, against the
floor, its steady rhythm stopping at the side of her bed.

Lying on her stomach, head in folded arms, blankets bunched
around her body and half over her head, Phaira opened one eye,
searching out the blurry silhouette of her brother. "What?"

"Okay, so don't fight me right away on this - "

She let out a growl of frustration, pulling the pillow over her
head. She'd only gotten back to the *Arazura* late last night, and
her body was worn to the bone. "Ren, come on," she hollered
into the mattress. "I'm tired, can't it wait?"

She felt the bed jostle; he'd kicked it in response. "Come on,
this is serious. You remember Theron Sava?"

"Yeah," Phaira mumbled, as her heart pounded in her ears
in the darkness.

"Well, he's in some trouble."

"So what?"

"And I've been thinking - "

"Ren, isn't that the job description when you're the head of a
criminal syndicate?" she interrupted him, lifting the pillow just
enough so her angry voice would carry. "To be a target? Why
do you care?"

"Because it's worse than all of that."

71

With a heavy exhale, Phaira pried open her eyes and tossed the pillow aside. "What, are you following his activities now?" she yawned.

"It's hard to avoid the rumors," Renzo said. "Then Jetsun called me."

"What?" Phaira exclaimed, pushing up onto her forearms. "His cousin called you? For what?"

"For help. Jetsun is scared. Four murders, all people close to him, and brutal by the sounds of it."

"So what does she want with you?"

"Not me," Renzo corrected. "You."

She kept her face neutral. "What is she asking?"

"If you'd come to Lea and be his bodyguard while they sort all this out."

With a twist in her stomach, Phaira recalled when he'd met her in Liera. That was his excuse for the incident in Honorwell; she was auditioning to be his bodyguard. She'd refused outright to work for him, to have any part of his life, how many times now? Now here it was again...

Is it such a surprise? Her mind scolded. *It always comes back to this.*

"I'll go, too. Help to figure out who is doing this," she heard Renzo add. "If we just stay on the outskirts..."

Phaira covered her face with her hands, rubbing the skin to wake up. "You want to get involved with the Savas," she mumbled through her fingers. "I can't believe I'm hearing this."

"Yeah, he's a Sava, but he's a decent guy," Renzo said. "He's helped us out a lot, and he's never asked for anything in return."

So you think, she wanted to say, but kept her mouth shut. Instead, she studied her brother. Renzo was agitated, more than she could remember in a long time.

"I agree with Renzo."

CaLarca's voice wafted through the room. Now mobile after severe injury, she still wore the leg braces that Renzo invented for stability, though she had progressed to a cane over crutches. She had grown leaner in the two months since Phaira was gone, her eyes even larger, taking everything in. Schemes running behind those black irises. Phaira could tell.

"We should help Theron Sava," CaLarca finished.

"You're a renter," Phaira said. "Your opinion is irrelevant."

"Stop that," Renzo chastised his sister.

Phaira gestured at CaLarca. "What do you call her butting in?" she exclaimed. "This is a private conversation."

"One that I'd like to be a part of," CaLarca said. "If you are proposing that Theron Sava is in need of protection, I wish to volunteer."

Renzo and Phaira gaped at her.

"Why?" Phaira finally asked, reluctantly pushing her body up to a sitting position.

"For the same reason as Renzo," CaLarca said. "I owe him."

"And what would you offer, exactly?" Phaira said, jerking her chin at CaLarca's braces.

CaLarca tilted her head. "Clearly, something that the two of you cannot."

Phaira's mind turned with the possibilities. It wasn't the worst idea, looking at it logically. Phaira had the physical prowess; Renzo the tech and travel skills; CaLarca would be able to pick up what their natural senses and mechanics could not. It was perfect, really. The ideal, well-rounded team.

But it couldn't happen. She didn't trust CaLarca, and she never would. There was something cold and exacting about the woman that put Phaira on edge. And she didn't believe CaLarca when she said she wanted to repay a debt to Theron. The last time she wanted to do that, Sydel had a near-nervous breakdown...

"It's a meeting," Renzo broke in. "To determine how we might get involved. No commitment, not yet. And if we decide to move forward, we'll be paid."

"With Sava money?" Phaira interjected. "Are you crazy?"

"Jetsun says she'll pay us out of her own pocket. All legal. She's scared, Phaira. I don't particularly like her, but I believe her. I don't think she'd reach out unless she were desperate."

Is he? she wondered. *Is he scared? Does he want me there, too?*

Phaira stared at her hands, the little scars on the palms and fingers, the scratches from travel, the dirt under her fingernails. It wasn't an ideal way to connect with Theron Sava again, but it was a way inside, under the cover of business. And she was tempted, too tempted, by the mystery, the more Renzo explained the events of the past few weeks. With everything that happened: no public response from Theron, not a word, not an appearance, not a hint of retaliation? Even the Lea patrol had an open investigation on the four dead Savas.

"How do we go about this?" she asked Renzo.

"We just show up. His security will let us through. I can get us there in three hours."

"He doesn't know we're coming?"

"Jet thought it was better this way."

How much power did Jetsun Sava hold over Theron, anyways?

"Phair," Renzo interrupted her thoughts. "I know it's crazy. I know it's dangerous, and in any other circumstances, we'd stay far, far away. I just - he's done a lot for us, you know? Helping to build the *Arazura*, and my prosthetic. Warning Cohen away from Keller. He and I built those HALOs together, and look how much they helped. He's technically a Sava, but he's been decent to us. If we can help, we should. It's the right thing to do."

It made sense. It terrified her, and it made her want to run away, but she couldn't deny the logic. And Renzo and CaLarca were in, incredibly. It was a team, like she always wanted. So tempting. So dangerous.

"All right," Phaira said. "Just a conversation. No commitments yet." She glanced over at CaLarca, who had been waiting silently all this time. "A moment, Ren?"

Renzo understood. His prosthetic clicked away, heading in the direction of the cockpit. The two women were alone.

"What did you find?" CaLarca's voice was soft.

"As you saw on satellite," Phaira confirmed. "Arson. Not much left. No sign of who set the fire. Damage was localized." As she spoke, she wondered if she should mention there were no signs of human remains.

"What else?" The woman seemed to be bracing herself.

"I spoke to your neighbor," Phaira said. "He didn't see anything. And I didn't find any evidence to offer any answers on why it happened. Or where your family is."

CaLarca nodded.

"I did find something in the rubble," Phaira added. Learning over the edge of her bed, she fished the bead out of her pants pocket, which were coiled in a heap on the floor. Then she lobbed it at the green-haired woman.

CaLarca caught it with a snap. "What is this?" she asked, staring at the bead.

"That's not yours?"

With disdain, CaLarca tossed the bead back at Phaira. "Have you nothing else to tell me? After all that time gone?"

Phaira's temper flared. "I did you a favor, going so far south.

You said you would be able to find things that we could not as a twosome," CaLarca fumed. "I believed you, and I've waited all this time for answers. This is ridiculous."

"Then get out of here," Phaira snapped. "Get off the *Arazura* and go figure it out yourself. I'm done."

She flopped backwards on her bed, turning her head to the wall.

Soon, the sound of CaLarca's stumbling footsteps grew faint, then disappeared.

* * *

The elevator ride was excruciating. Jetsun was insistent; she would arrange a private conversation between Theron and Renzo, CaLarca, and Phaira. They would go to his apartment, under cover of night, and surprise him at the door, with no outside interference.

So far, Jetsun was true to her word. There were no guards posted in the lobby of the skyscraper, housed in the south end of Lea. No bodyguard checked their identification or frisked them before they got into the elevator. The ride to the penthouse was silent. Phaira noted that the cameras in the corner were taped over. No record of their presence.

The elevator opened. At the end of a long white hallway, which carried the pinching stink of bleach, there was a black door.

Above the doorframe, a Lissome swiveled on its base, taking in each of their faces. Phaira kept her expression neutral, as she held onto every fiber of her skin to remain still. Annoyingly, his name kept repeating in her head. *Theron. Theron. Theron.*

The door opened, and his silhouette filled the frame. Six and a half feet tall, black hair tied back, sharp cheekbones, full mouth, amber eyes. For a moment, Phaira could only register how hot the skin at the base of her throat felt. He'd lost weight. He had circles under his eyes.

But he wouldn't look at her, nor Renzo or CaLarca, who stood next to her. Instead he glared at the floor and grumbled, "Jetsun called you."

"Can we come in?" Renzo asked, moving as if to push past Theron.

But Theron blocked the way. "No."

"Why?" Phaira challenged, before she could stop herself.

The condescension in his voice rattled her. "I don't have to explain myself to you."

Stupid, came those familiar thoughts. *Stupid, stupid....*

"Let us in."

Still stinging, Phaira glanced over her shoulder. CaLarca leaned on her cane, but her black gaze was unblinking.

Theron's face twisted. "You," he spat, "get out of my sight."

CaLarca had no reaction. "I have come to help you."

"Help me?"

"Indeed," CaLarca said, her voice like a shiver of ice. "So let us in."

Long seconds passed. Theron's angry breathing was audible.

Then the giant man stepped aside, to Phaira's surprise. Did CaLarca use her Eko to sway him to move? Was that possible? She didn't want to consider it.

When she walked past Theron into the apartment, he stiffened and stepped back. Mortified, Phaira let her blue hair fall over her face, and pushed her hands in her pockets, wishing she could fall through the floor. She shouldn't have come. Why had she listened to Renzo?

As the door clicked shut, Phaira took in the great, silent living space: brown, scarlet and black, dark and stuffy, expensive and uncomfortable. Nothing like the house by the cliffs, except for the weaponry displayed on the wall. She recognized the katana blade, the one she'd taken for defense, and later returned to Theron in that park garden, so many weeks ago.

CaLarca shuffled around the perimeter. With her spare hand, she ran her long thin fingers along the edge of the sofa. Her green-streaked braids swung across the centerline of her back. Theron watched her the entire while.

Next to Phaira, Renzo crossed his arms, addressing Theron. "Well? Tell us what's going on."

Theron scowled. "I brought you inside to tell you the way out," he said through gritted teeth. "Leave, single file, minutes apart. Use the rear emergency staircase. Don't come here again."

Phaira had the impulse to grab hold of Theron, to shake him, to force him to look at her. Instead, she kept her head down as the two men argued.

"Let us help you."

"I never asked for your help, or her help."

"She can keep you from getting killed, for starters."

"What do any of you care?" Theron's eyes flicked over to CaLarca, who was completing her slow turn around the room.

"What is with you?" Renzo snapped. "You were fine the last time I saw you."

"The last time?" Phaira interrupted. "This isn't your first meeting on this?"

Both men's faces held the same guilty look for a second, before Theron's face hardened, and Renzo threw up his hands in exasperation. "We were talking business – at the time, it - "

"Give me a minute alone with him," Phaira insisted.

"What? Why?" Renzo demanded.

Phaira caught Theron's eye. "If Jetsun wants me to protect him. If I'm putting my body and the two of you at risk, we need to understand each other."

She glanced at her older brother. "So, please. One minute."

CaLarca's black eyes flitted between Theron and Phaira. Then she limped over and took Renzo's arm. "We will wait on the balcony," she announced.

When the glass door sealed, and their backs were turned, Phaira faced Theron. He wasn't looking at her, still. She kept six feet of space between them. She couldn't read his expression, cast in shadows.

"You look terrible, you know," she echoed his words, said so long ago, it seemed.

Theron didn't react. He was watching CaLarca through the window.

"You should know that I don't trust her, and I never will."

He broke his glare to glance at her.

Phaira raised her eyebrows. "It wasn't my choice to get her involved. But CaLarca is a resource, and she's willing. So use it to your advantage."

"You sound like Jetsun." There was disgust in his voice.

"Then I guess..." Phaira paused, stumbling over her words. "I guess she cares about what happens to you, too."

His voice was a bite. "I doubt that."

Her heart dropped to her feet. Did the hurt show on her face? She refused to let it. "I'm not begging to get involved here," she said sharply. "If you want to get killed, so be it. But I can keep you alive until you find out who's doing this."

"That's not what's happening here," Theron shot back.

He gestured for Renzo and CaLarca to come back inside. The two emerged from the balcony, windblown and red-cheeked.

"So?" Renzo probed. "Are we doing this?"

"Let's be clear," Theron said curtly, addressing the three of them. "This assassin is targeting people in my circle. I haven't been touched."

"Not yet," Phaira pointed out.

"The people near me are the ones at risk," Theron said, ignoring her. "You stay here, you'll get killed."

Phaira said nothing. She was the offensive force in this trio; was she really ready to be the open target for this assassin, whoever it was? Was she ready to see Renzo in the same position?

"Well," Renzo began. "I'd say it's up to the girls. But I'm willing to stay and help to figure this out. There's a lot of areas we can look into."

"As will I," CaLarca said, her expression neutral, as always. "I owe you a debt, Theron Sava."

His repulsion was palatable. "I have no use for your favors."

"Oh?" CaLarca countered, the edge back in her voice. "I can hear the whispers out of your earshot. I can see who is lying, and who is afraid. Can you use that kind of information?"

Theron's mouth twisted.

Renzo glanced at Phaira, a question in his eyes. *Well?*

Phaira clenched her jaw. "I'll do it," she finally confirmed. "I'll be your bodyguard. Until this is resolved."

Theron snorted. "You're as good as dead, then.

"Then so be it," Phaira shot back, more vehemently than she meant to. She felt CaLarca's curious gaze on her again.

"Fine," Theron finally huffed. "Fine. Stay. But just remember: I never asked you to."

Phaira resisted the urge to roll her eyes. *The drama. I forgot about that part of him.*

III.

The agreement made, the next step was to strategize. So the three *Arazura* residents took seats at the dining table. Theron remained standing, looking out of the balcony window.

"Why don't you just leave?" Phaira asked, when the silence grew too awkward. "Go into hiding?"

"Not an option," Theron said. "I have to keep every appointment. Show strength."

"Why?"

Renzo jostled her under the table. When she glowered at him, he gave her a pointed look, as if asking, *Why do you think?*

She couldn't help her snappish tone, though. She wanted to get a rise out of Theron, to pierce through that cold and figure out what was going on underneath.

"Your assassin is likely someone in your world," CaLarca said.

"No," Theron said, already distracted. "It doesn't fit."

"What do you mean, it doesn't fit?" Renzo asked, surprised. "You've already ruled them all out?"

"It's too violent."

"For the mob?" Phaira couldn't help but blurt out.

Theron shot her a look. Then he sighed and rubbed his face with his hand. "There are rules," he told the three. "Guns, sure. Beatings. A fall off a rooftop. People don't stray from what they know. But this is - this is animalistic. Done in public. Whoever this is, it's not the norm."

"Someone could have hired an outsider," Phaira pointed out.

"I'm assuming you've checked for bounty contracts," Renzo chimed in. "Both public and underground."

"I have," Theron said. "Nothing."

"Any personal feuds?" Renzo pressed. "Anyone looking to get even with you?"

"I'm not popular," was the only comment. "It could be anyone."

Phaira leaned over to murmur in Renzo's ear. "Maybe we should we ask Anandi to look into -"

"No," Theron interrupted. "I want to keep the circle tight. You talk to no one."

Phaira's temper flared. Why was he being such a pain? She had never seen him like this before. Sure, he was obnoxious that first night by the cliffs, when he was half drunk, but he wasn't malicious.

Control, she told herself. *Stay focused on the business at hand. He is your charge.*

"Well, you might refuse to go into hiding, but you can't stay in this apartment," Phaira announced, rising to her feet. "There's only one exit, too many blind spots, not to mention your building's security system is outdated. Locks and cameras aren't going to be enough. You need to be in a place where I can see you, at all times. Do you have any other properties? Any safe houses?"

"Not anymore."

Was he talking about the apartment in Liera, or the house in the cliffs in Karum? Were they both gone?

"The *Arazura*," Renzo broke in. "You should come onto the *Arazura*."

"Into your home?" Theron exclaimed.

Renzo shrugged. "It's mobile, which is better than here. And you know the design: top-of-the-line security measures." He turned to Phaira. "He can conduct meetings remotely, and we can scramble the cc so it can't be traced. Maybe CaLarca can put some kind of field or protection around the space."

Phaira didn't know what to say to that. There was something perverse about Theron staying on the *Arazura*; his fingerprints were already all over the ship, having secretly helped with its construction in a strange attempt to 'evaluate' her and her brothers months ago.

"That's not possible," Theron said quietly, surprising them all. "In fact, none of this is right. But I can't spend any more time on this. I have a function to attend."

"A function?" Renzo asked, wrinkling his brow. "What is that code for?"

"Charitable fundraiser." There was a faint smirk on Theron's face, the first shade of the man Phaira remembered. "Jetsun is a philanthropist. In one hour, there's a very important gathering of people, in a very expensive ballroom in the city, and if I don't show up, she'll take my head off."

"Well," Phaira said. "I guess that's my first test." Already, her mind was whirring; what she should bring, what she should research, what she should prepare herself for...

"You're not coming," Theron interrupted her thoughts.

Phaira glared at him. "I'm your bodyguard. Watch me."

"You don't know what you're asking."

"Again, wrong," Phaira sniped. "I want to lure this person out. If I'm with you in public, that's more likely to happen, isn't it?"

"You want to get attacked?"

"How else can I get a real sense of the situation?"

"Do you have a date?" CaLarca's voice startled them all. She'd been silent since they sat down, only her eyes following the conversation.

Theron's face darkened again. "There's a woman that Bianco had -" He paused for just a half-second before continuing. "Who was prearranged to accompany me."

"I see," CaLarca said. "I think you should take me, instead."

Renzo and Phaira were speechless. Theron looked like he might be physically sick.

"Let me explain," CaLarca said smoothly. "Phaira is your bodyguard; therefore, all eyes will be on her, because everyone knows that your guards have been targeted. That leaves their thoughts, their fears, and their secrets open and vulnerable, which I can sense if I am by your side. If someone is behind this, and actively plotting, I can use Eko to overhear it."

She turned to Renzo. "And Renzo can monitor the exits and security cameras in the safety of the *Arazura*, and warn us if there is any suspicious activity."

Theron's jaw worked. Phaira could sense his frustration; he was trying to think of something to counter the argument. But Phaira couldn't deny that it was a good plan, and she knew he couldn't either.

"I think you should do it," Renzo confirmed.

"There's a certain code of behavior expected at these events," Theron finally said.

"I can perform accordingly," CaLarca said. "A hired escort is always more efficient, is it not?"

Her cool logic was unnerving.

"I'll need something to wear, of course," she added.

"Jetsun can courier over something to wear," Theron said. "For both of you."

"I'm not wearing a ballgown," Phaira announced.

As soon as she spoke, a flush crept up the back of her neck. The first and only time she'd worn one, it was a borrowed gown: a silver-gray, strapless piece that was too big in the chest and threatened to slip down with every step. Theron had seen it; he said that it didn't suit her, she remembered, in the brief, tense moments at that party in Honorwell.

"No," Theron said. "No, nothing like that."

* * *

Within thirty minutes, a courier was in the lobby. In addition to a dress bag for CaLarca, Jetsun had sent over clothes for Phaira: white leggings, with leather strips and netting making subtle patterns in the fabric; a matching white jacket, slim and sharp, with folds along the shoulders; a dark silver camisole for underneath. Expensive, but practical for mobility, and fancy enough to fit into a formal event. Phaira was grateful that the woman didn't send her something awful and gaudy.

Then again, she mused, *if this was Jetsun's fundraiser, she will want everything to be perfect, and for everyone to be in their appropriate place. And the white's a conscious choice.*

If I'm the bodyguard to a syndicate man, then I have to look like one.

Phaira dressed quickly in Theron's bedroom, changing behind the half-closed door. A small mirror hung on the wall. Catching sight of her reflection, she slicked her hair back so it was off her face. Some pieces curled around her ears and throat; it was getting longer. She hadn't had it cut in ages. It was almost lying smooth now, like when she was in the army. Her eyes were large and glittering in the darkness, her mouth a smudge of shadow.

CaLarca soon emerged from the washroom. She wore a collar of silver leaves, open at the base of her throat. Her body a narrow black column and her shoulders exposed, her collarbones highlighted by her braids twisted at the back of her head. There was no sign of her leg braces underneath the gown, though she held her cane still, and leaned on it heavily. But she was stunning, and everyone in the apartment was surprised to see it.

She'll fit in easily, Phaira realized. In fact, CaLarca and Theron looked good together. He was in all black as well, a slim-cut suit with no lapels, his grey wool overcoat and leather gloves already on, his hair neatly tied back. Still striking. Dammit.

"Are we ready?" CaLarca asked.

From afar, Phaira saw the struggle in Theron's face, and wondered if he were to attack CaLarca, what she would do in response. And vice versa. Finally, he opened the front door.

Holding the edge, he curtly gestured for CaLarca to go. She glided past him into the hallway.

Maybe if we are lucky, Phaira thought, *people will mistake Theron's hatred of his date for sexual tension.*

"Are you coming?" Theron's voice broke into her thoughts.

"What can I carry into this place?" she asked under her breath.

He understood what she meant, though his expression remained cold. "No guns allowed. Jetsun's rule."

Then Theron's gaze went to the katana, displayed on his apartment wall. "Your choice," he added, before turning crisply on his heel and exiting.

With a sigh, Phaira walked over to the wall and removed the blade. Still sharp, still light as she remembered, from back in the house on the cliffs. When she slid it into the black sheath, there was a faint, whispering sound as they came together. A strange comfort, somehow, held horizontally in her hand. Familiar.

She touched her finger to the Lissome piece, affixed just under her ear. "Heading out, Ren."

"I'm here," came his response. "I'm watching."

* * *

When they entered the ballroom, the crowd shushed. As Theron walked, his face dark, with CaLarca's hand in the crook of his elbow, whispers floated behind their backs.

Though Theron ignored every curious face, CaLarca smiled at the onlookers. Her face changed when she smiled, Phaira noted, it was luminous. Her cane swung like a natural limb, an elegant accessory.

By comparison, Phaira remained six feet behind, taking in the scene: black, silver, gold, glitter, floor-length silken gowns, sharp lapels, plunging necklines. She looked for any sign of bulkiness under jackets, any tiny squares or devices hidden under great towers of hair. The cloying smell of flowers and vanilla, the sounds of a string orchestra in the background. Chandeliers glittered overhead, highlighting the floor-to-ceiling windows with stained-glass designs. Staff dressed in black and white ducked in and out of the space.

And there was Jetsun in the middle of it all. The skirt of her white dress was voluminous, but her sleeveless top was composed of pearls, looping around her neck and shoulders, and then drooping in rows all the way down her naked back. Her hair had been teased to great height at the front, then slicked into a series of completed twists and knots at the back. Her mouth was red and laughing, as she held a glass of champagne to her lips.

Then she caught sight of Theron, Phaira and CaLarca.

Setting down her glass, she eyed the group with interest. Then she approached with hips swinging.

When she arrived, Theron leaned over so she could kiss the air next to his cheek. Her mountain of hair never moved, Phaira noted. It was impressive.

Jetsun surveyed CaLarca. "Hm," was her only remark.

"You look very nice," she told Theron. "Stay for one hour, and then you can go."

Then, surprisingly, Jetsun embraced Phaira. Her warm perfume, peach and plum notes, was a stark contrast to her icy whisper in Phaira's ear: "No fidgeting."

"I didn't realize we were so close," Phaira said wryly as they pulled apart.

"I'm showing my public approval, you twit," Jetsun smiled, taking her hand. "And my gratitude."

"Oh, is that it?" Phaira said, itching to yank her fingers away. "Will the rest of your clan feel the same way, I wonder?"

"No one will give you trouble," Jetsun said, casting a bright grin at someone in the distance.

Is she that powerful? Phaira wondered, fighting the urge to inspect her surroundings. *Maybe she's the real head of the syndicate, not Theron...*

"Tomorrow morning," Jetsun said through her smiling teeth. "I'll expect you at my office to talk strategy. In the meantime, don't be alone with him."

And before Phaira could respond, Jetsun released her hand and flounced away, her dress swished across the ballroom floor, the pearls making gentle clicking noises.

At her movement, music began to play again, a slow, romantic waltz. Couples paired off. Phaira remained on the edge, by the round tables, as Theron took CaLarca's hand and drew her into the center of the dance floor.

"Do you recognize her?" Phaira heard the whispers all around. "Where does he find these girls?" "Ten rana says this one doesn't last the night." She listened as she catalogued the world before her, around her, above her. Any of these eyes on her back could be affixing a target. There was something thrilling about it. She had no doubt that, whoever this assailant was, she could handle them. And the sooner this was resolved, the better.

"Would you like to sit down?"

At the voice, Phaira glanced to her right. Sitting at the nearest round table, the elderly woman glittered with diamonds, her white hair combed back in a dramatic sweep. She gestured at Phaira to join her.

Phaira shook her head. "Working." She placed her hand on the hilt of her katana, strapped to her waist.

"I see that," the woman said. "You're the new bodyguard."

Phaira said nothing, keeping her eyes on Theron's broad back. He was a lousy dancer, she noted with amusement, mostly just rocking back and forth with stiff legs. When he turned, she could see the delicate line of CaLarca's exposed spine, and his tense hand, holding court just below her ribs. Their lips were moving, first Theron, then CaLarca's. Phaira could see the veins in his throat.

Then they separated. Audible murmurs rose as Theron cut through the crowd, leaving CaLarca on the floor.

He was headed straight for Phaira.

She lifted her chin and held her breath, staring him down as he approached, ready for the confrontation.

He didn't acknowledge her, though, as he slid into a chair at the table . "Hello," he said, flashing a smile across the table at the diamond woman. "Can I sit here?"

"Oh!" the woman gasped, delighted by the attention. "How lovely. Of course, Mr. Sava."

"Having a wonderful time?" There was mockery in the way he said those words.

Phaira fought the urge to sigh, and kept her gaze on the dance floor. CaLarca had been taken up by another man; that familiar, pinched look was back on her face.

"It's breathtaking," the woman was saying. "Ms. Jetsun has such a talent."

"Indeed she does," Theron said. "Don't you think so, Phaira?"

Phaira ignored him.

"I must say, Mr. Sava," the woman whispered, a delighted lilt in her voice. "It's surprising that you are working with a woman protector. However did you come across her?"

"Oh, her?" His tone was light and playful, utterly different from the one Phaira knew. "We used to date."

Phaira smirked at that, despite her better instincts.

"Really!" the woman exclaimed with delight.

"Oh yes," Theron said, leaning back like a lord. "A long time ago."

Phaira felt his shoulder near her hip. On purpose?

"And you're still able to work together?" The question was ripe with curiosity. "How special!"

"In-deed." The word was drawn out, a sly note in the syllables. Phaira gritted her teeth.

"Since you brought it to light, I must ask," the woman continued eagerly. "Why did you break up?"

At the edge of her vision, Phaira saw Theron's arm move. She heard the tiniest rustle from under the table. Then she stiffened as his fingers grazed the outside of her knee.

"Why do you think?" he murmured over his shoulder, up to her.

He was trying to embarrass her. He was trying to make her react.

As his fingertips made lazy patterns along the back of her thigh, Phaira turned her head.

"Bad timing," she told the woman coolly.

Theron gave an amused *hmph!* The heat of his hand receded.

The woman looked confused. Then she nodded, her lips pursed, as if she understood. "Oh yes," she agreed. "Timing is everything in life, isn't it? One opportunity, there and gone -"

"If you'll excuse us," Phaira interrupted. "Mr. Sava is required elsewhere."

"Am I?" Theron asked, leaning his head back and grinning up at her.

It was too much. "Get up," she ordered.

"You dare to speak to me like that?" Theron drawled.

"That and more," Phaira hissed. "Now, before I make a scene."

Chuckling, Theron unfolded his long body from his seat. When he stood upright, he loomed over everyone in the room. "Excuse me," he told the woman. "My girl is upset with me."

Furious, Phaira grabbed his elbow and steered him through the tables to where she'd seen the signs for private washrooms. She heard his voice trailing behind her, addressing the shocked onlookers: "This is why you don't hire a woman for this kind of thing...."

Inside the lavatory, a couple leapt away from each other, half-undressed, as Phaira shoved Theron through the door.

"Out!" Phaira hollered at them.

The couple quickly adjusted straps and buttons, and ran out of the space.

As the door swung shut, Theron sauntered across the red carpet, past the great, gilded mirror and chaise lounge, to take a seat in a plush red chair. "If you can't handle your charge, maybe you should just cut and run," he announced, in that infuriating, smirky tone.

Phaira dead-bolted the door and whirled around to glare at him. She jabbed a finger in his direction. "Stop acting like a brat to push me away."

His features twisted. "Then stop playing games with me."

"Me?" Phaira exclaimed. "Who's acting like a complete -"

"I know who you work for, Phaira." His tone was bitter. "What does Ozias want you to bring back? I'll just tell you what you need to know, save you the trouble of pretending any longer."

Phaira stared at him. Hurt struck her like an arrow. *Personal and professional*, her conscience reminded her. *See what happens when you let them mix?*

"I was threatened with jail time..." she began.

He slumped into his chair. "So you don't deny it," he muttered. "How could you?"

She ignored him, and continued. "... for assaulting the patrol in Liera. So I made a deal with Ozias to investigate the remaining NINE."

Theron frowned, taken aback. "NINE?"

"Yes. I've been East and South for the past three months. I just got back to the *Arazura* yesterday." She held his gaze.

"And you know plenty of my secrets, so why would I ever share yours?"

Theron was silent. Watching him, her heart thumped. She had the sudden urge to step inside his knees, to slide her cheek against his. She could remember the sensation of his breath on her neck....

Then her vision blurred. Phaira shook her head to clear it. But the room was getting darker, the light tinted orange. Then pink, and even deeper as she blinked.

Was she passing out?

Her memory sparked: maybe some kind of gas was being pumped into the ventilation systems, like Huma did so many months ago, trying to knock them out....

"Red." She heard him gasp, heard his boots on the floor. "It's here."

He saw the colors too?

Then she remembered Jetsun's warning.

They were alone.

"Stay back," she ordered, running to stand before him, her right hand drawing the katana, her left arm outstretched in a horizontal barrier as she swept the area. But her mind was slowing, and her stomach was in knots, and something was pulling her, every bit of her, towards the ground, like weights attached to every pore of her skin.

Phaira scoured the room again for signs of movement, for a third person's breath, but the world was growing red, and her hands were ice, and there was an odd, creaking sound repeating itself in the back of her mind...

The door handle rattled.

Suddenly, Phaira's vision went clear and bright again, as if someone turned up the lights.

Then the washroom door opened, revealing a slim metal pick, white hands, green braids and black satin. "What's going on in here?" CaLarca hissed.

"Why are you breaking in?" Phaira shot back, lowering her blade.

Bodies loomed behind CaLarca; a crowd had gathered, little whispers filtering through.

"It's gone," came Theron's voice, so quiet that only Phaira could hear.

"We need to leave," Phaira announced.

CaLarca led them through the ballroom. Theron followed four steps behind Phaira. He didn't break stride, even when she heard Jetsun's protesting voice, growing fainter.

The night air was a release, soaked with the promise of rain. Phaira caught sight of a glimmer, one hundred feet away: the *Arazura*, and CaLarca, her pale skin highlighted by the moon, striding to the open entryway.

"Come on," Phaira said to Theron over her shoulder. "It's the best place for right now."

She could barely hear his soft response. "I'm sorry."

Phaira didn't know what to say to that, so she propelled forward. When she reached the *Arazura*, she stepped to the side and kept her eyes on the ground. CaLarca stood on the other side of the hatch.

Theron hesitated at the entryway, before ducking his head and pulling himself through. Inside, she heard Renzo greeting Theron, already asking questions.

"This is a bad idea," Phaira muttered.

"Why's that?" came CaLarca's cool voice.

When Phaira glanced up, CaLarca was studying her with curiosity. Phaira lifted her chin. "Did you see the red, too?"

"You saw red?"

"We both did."

CaLarca looked thoughtful. "I didn't. That's strange."

"I just assumed that's why you broke open the door."

"It was locked," CaLarca said dryly. "You were alone in there, and Jetsun was panicking. What were you two doing?"

"Making peace," Phaira said.

"Peace," CaLarca repeated.

Phaira scowled. "Get inside," she ordered. "And take that stupid dress off."

CaLarca's bemused expression remained as she stepped into the *Arazura*, her cane clicking alongside her high heels.

IV

I saw lies. Everyone in the room had a sheen of grey. One of the most dismal sights I've ever seen."

"You can 'see' lies?" Theron broke in. He was wandering the perimeter of the *Arazura* common space, running his hand over the walls. He hadn't seen the end product, yet, Phaira realized, just the internal guts, when he was helping Renzo with construction.

"Do you wish to test me?" CaLarca asked. She was back in one of her regular tunics, her braids loose down her back, her SCKAFO leggings shimmering under the light.

"Focus, please," Phaira said from the end of the table. She'd removed the borrowed jacket to get some air over her arms and clear her head. "What did you sense?"

"A definite sense of foreboding," CaLarca said. "And some fear."

Theron huffed. Phaira wondered why. "What about anger?" she asked. "Hatred? Evil plotting?"

"Nothing so unusual," CaLarca said. "Everyone was varying levels of intoxicated. Alcohol tends to stir up emotions. Nothing violent directed at Theron, or -"

"Any animosity towards me?" Phaira interjected.

"Just curiosity. A few people knew your name and seemed impressed. Can't imagine why."

CaLarca shrugged. "There is the question, however," she added, "of the red vision you and Theron experienced. How did it make you feel?"

Phaira and Theron exchanged looks.

"Like a filter," Phaira said, passing her hand over her face. "Everything went deep red, like blood. And everything felt heavy, like gravity had increased."

"Did you feel that too?" CaLarca asked Theron. "Visual distortion and pressure?"

The man gave the slightest nod.

"And?" CaLarca pressed. "More than that?"

Phaira heard a faint squeak; it was his right hand, tightening on the edge of his seat. "Some kind of repeating noise," Theron muttered. "A hiss, or a word or - something - inside my head."

So they had experienced the same thing.

"Sounds like an Eko," came Renzo's voice from the doorway. He'd finally left the cockpit and stood at an angle, surveying the group in the common room.

"You think it's NINE?" Phaira asked her brother.

Renzo jerked his chin at CaLarca. "Sounds like she thinks it is."

CaLarca held up her hand. "Not necessarily from my original group," she corrected. "But someone with enhanced abilities, it's very possible. Though I would have sensed it, I'm sure."

"Well, who's left?" Phaira pushed. "Who is still out there and alive?

"Zarek Voss," CaLarca listed. "Shantou Lyung."

She went to speak another name, but closed her mouth.

A call came in, then. Renzo waved his hand at the console to make the connection. A woman's rushed whisper floated through the space. "We've got bodies downstairs: a man and a woman. The same as the others. It's a mess, and everyone is still here. If they find out, the media will be everywhere, and law, and my reputation - "

Jetsun, Phaira realized. She opened her mouth to call out to the woman, but Theron beat her to it. "Jet, who made the discovery?"

"One of ours. He had the sense of mind to get me right away."

"Make an announcement," Theron ordered, his voice surprisingly calm. "Tell the guests that there is a plumbing issue. They'll all find excuses to leave, no one will want to take the risk in any of the washrooms. Offer refunds, as requested. If the building owner is present, pay him off. Then secure the area, lock down the cameras and any other security devices. If you suspect any other witnesses, isolate them."

Phaira couldn't help but stare at him as he talked. "Theron," she said.

He glanced at her, his black eyebrows knitted together.

"Can we get in and look before the - the clean-up?" She forced the last word out, resisting the urge to wince. Her mind was spinning. They were getting into dangerous territory. Delaying the law. Bribing witnesses. Was it worth it, just to find a murderer? She wasn't sure.

Still, Theron nodded. "We're on our way back, Jet," he announced. "No one from outside until we get there."

Phaira caught Renzo's eye. *Is that okay?* she asked with her expression.

He had a sick look on his face, but he nodded.

"Everyone wears a HALO," he told the group as he headed back to the *Arazura* cockpit. "No exceptions."

* * *

Jetsun was wrapped in a thick gray coat, but visibly shivering. Her blonde hair was falling from its bouffant, her make-up smeared under her eyes, her mouth drawn in a tight line. On exiting the *Arazura*, Phaira caught the silent exchange between her and Theron.

Then Jetsun ducked her head and led them back inside the hotel, her head turning left and right the whole while. Phaira did the same, as did CaLarca. She knew Renzo was doing the same, inside the safety of the *Arazura*, scanning for any signs of danger.

Inside, the ballroom was deserted, littered with confetti and napkins. The candles had burnt down to almost nothing, the tablecloths half-hanging off the tables. Phaira felt the soles of her boots sticking to spots on the wooden floor. *Things must have gotten crazy after we left*, she mused. *Who knew philanthropists were so wild?*

Jetsun led them down a marble staircase, where there was more activity in the lower level; the wait staff cleaning up, cracks of light seeping through closed doors. Next to her, CaLarca had a strange look on her face, her head tilted as she looked around. Theron lingered at the rear of the group, but Phaira couldn't read his expression.

Jetsun stopped in front of a door. From her coat pocket, she produced a skeleton key, brass and intricate, and fit it into the lock. Then Jetsun leaned back, checking to see that no new eyes were watching them, before she opened the door.

Inside, two bodies were sprawled across the floor, a young man and woman. Blood soaked the floor. There were spatters on the wall, too.

Phaira was the first to enter. She knelt down, breathing through the side of her mouth to avoid the copper stink, to get a closer look. Both victims' faces had been slashed, four jagged lines across, eyes sagging, lips torn. Then the throat, hitting the jugular vein. And finally the belly, purple, ropy intestines peeking through the sequined dress and cummerbund. Also jagged. Same weapon? What kind?

When she glanced at their faces again, a jolt of recognition coursed through her. The jeweled comb in the woman's hair. The cufflinks on the man.

The lovers in the washroom, the ones scrambling to redress, who ran out at Phaira's command.

She'd sent the two in search of another hiding place. Downstairs, away from the guests, they were easy targets in this closet, with so much noise from the kitchen, the music and the ballroom. No one would hear them screaming....

"Is this...." Her voice sounded so odd in the silence. "Is this like the others?" she finally managed, turning to search for Theron.

His silhouette filled the doorframe. One hand was in his suit pocket. One hand, however, was in constant motion, his fingertips touching, again and again, as though he were trying to conjure something.

"Faces, no," Theron said. "Throats, yes."

Next to him, Jetsun's hand covered her mouth, like she was stifling vomit. Was she that sensitive? Then again, it was a different matter to see death in front of you, already decomposing....

"But they weren't your protection detail," CaLarca broke in. "They were just guests, right? Do you know them?"

Theron shook his head. When he glanced over at Jetsun, she lifted one shoulder. "I recall their faces, I think," she said weakly. "I don't know their names. I haven't looked for identification yet."

Her face scrunched up suddenly. "Wait - is that a heart on the wall?"

Theron stiffened, as if shot.

Catching his surprise, Phaira turned to peer where Jetsun was pointing. CaLarca had already crouched down, one hand on the far wall to steady herself, the other gripping her cane. Phaira squinted; there it was, just as Jetsun said, the shape of a heart, drawn in blood and already dry. It had been done in a quick swipe, no drips, Phaira noted. She could make out a thin line in the center of the trail. Someone used their finger to do this?

"Have you seen this before?" she asked over her shoulder. "Theron?"

Theron's mouth moved, but he didn't make any sound. Finally, he turned on his heel and strode out of the room.

Jetsun went to follow, but Phaira stopped her. "Tell the truth," she ordered. "Is this some kind of girlfriend's sick revenge?"

"I can't imagine," Jetsun sputtered. "The ones he's been with, they don't have the capacity to do such a thing."

"But they could hire someone," Phaira pointed out.

"I suppose, yes, but we've searched in the network, there's no contract listing, no trace of any kind of transaction that suggests - and it's so risky, given his position - who would ever consider this kind of aggressive action, knowing who he is?"

Everyone was silent, considering her words.

"What will you do now?" CaLarca was the first to speak as she wobbled up to her feet. "Will you allow these two to be claimed by their families?"

"That's up to Theron," Jetsun said.

"It's in question?" CaLarca spat, surprising Phaira. "These two are barely adults. Their families will be devastated."

Jetsun lifted her chin. "Consider the world you're in right now, whatever your name is. The family comes first. Always. And that applies to outside employees."

A warning, Phaira thought wearily. *Always a warning.* For the thousandth time, she wondered why she had agreed to be involved.

A scream carried like a shockwave from outside the room.

Then the lights shorted out.

The door slammed shut, and the storage room plunged into darkness.

"No!" Jetsun gasped.

Phaira's heart thudded, one hand gripping the katana at her hip, one hand in front of her to feel. They were the only ones in the space. She felt CaLarca's cool form to her right, and Jetsun's shuddering one to her left.

But Theron is outside.

"Stay with Jetsun," she ordered CaLarca's shadow. "Don't let anyone in."

When Phaira burst outside, the hallway was dark. Next door, the kitchen was silent. But there were shadows moving, the sound of breathing, the smell of sweat. And the color red, floating in front of her eyes.

Twenty feet down the corridor, two bodies struggled against the wall. A flash of metal. Then a gurgling sound, and an exhalation. A giant silhouette slumped to the floor, his head flopped back, his legs folded under him. The other stood over Theron's body, unmoving, swathed in darkness from head to toe.

Theron, she realized. *I'm too late.*

The blood roared in Phaira's ears, and her muscles felt like they would explode, but her mind was slowing down, settling into focus.

Another glint in the darkness: metal again, where the assailant's hands lay at their thighs. Metal tips. Yes, that made sense; right to left, swiping motions to kill and maim. Was it an animal before her? There was something on the ground between them, something glimmering. A handgun, a gold one. Theron's? Had he snuck one in, after all?

Then, with a crackle, the figure vanished.

Stunned, Phaira swiveled in place, hunting.

The sound of skittering, like tiny metal taps, rattled over her head.

A thump behind her.

Phaira swung her blade in an arc, and caught resistance, fabric, maybe skin.

The world shimmered, the crackling sound returned, and the assassin was suddenly in front of her, its hot, rotten breath overpowering, metal mask, metal claws in sharp focus, body and head swathed in deep red, attacking.

Phaira slid out of the way, rolling to grab the handgun on the floor, prime it and fire at the beast. But the trigger wouldn't budge. She smacked it with the side of her hand. Jammed?

Didn't matter. When the assailant leapt, she defended, deflecting every swipe of the metal claws, trying to keep it at a distance as she searched for soft spots. But there was no time to collect details; the creature was fast. A horizontal swipe almost connected with her face, had Phaira not anticipated and arched back, the swish of air in front of her.

Then a boot suddenly connected with Phaira's knee and her leg collapsed, leaving her left ribs exposed. In the split second of vulnerability, she braced for the white flash of pain. She was dead. She was bleeding out. She had failed.

But the red assassin didn't advance. Phaira could hear its breath rattling through the metal mask. Was it looking at her, as she stumbled?

Then the red assailant shimmered out of sight, the crackling sound overwhelmed by the sound of sirens.

"No!" Phaira yelled, stumbling to her feet, swiping with her katana, searching desperately.

She ran down one hallway, and then to the other end. Gone.

Theron was still slumped against the wall, his hands splayed, his face awash with blood. Phaira threw aside her blade and ran her hands over his body, his legs, his arms, his torso, searching for gaping wounds, for hot blood or compound fractures. But, miraculously, he seemed intact. And he breathed; she could hear the ragged intake and exhale.

"You're alive!"

The voice came from Jetsun, who had emerged from the closet, while CaLarca hobbled behind. Then Jetsun let out a cry as she caught sight of Theron on the floor.

"He's okay, I think," Phaira told the woman, holding up a hand, hoping it didn't shake. "It's over."

"You didn't die." Jetsun kept repeating, as if disbelieving.

No, Phaira admitted to herself, working to calm her breath. *Not this time.*

* * *

As the *Arazura* took to the sky, and finally switched to autopilot, Renzo proceeded to change every registration, connection code, theory and mention of them in the public network. He activated a shield around the *Arazura* that Phaira hadn't known about, one that would detect any foreign presence or infiltration. Up in the sky, at least, they were safe. Phaira didn't know where they should go next, but as long as they stayed off the ground, she could concentrate on her superficial wounds and go over the details of what happened with Renzo.

Theron's head wound was not as bad as it looked, just a deep gash across the forehead. He was otherwise unhurt. Now Theron and Jetsun had shut themselves away in the *Arazura's* lower training area. Phaira didn't have the energy to barge in and insist that she be a part of the conversation they were likely having. So she had CaLarca stand watch, with instructions to let Phaira know when they emerged again.

In the meantime, Phaira had Renzo's full attention as he tended to her wounds in her cabin. When she removed her shirt sleeves, her arms were crisscrossed with scratches, some pink, some red, some white from the fight. Her knee ached.

If Sydel were here, Phaira thought, wincing, *she could wave her hand and everything would be gone and painless.*

But she wasn't, so it was back to the tried-and-true method of iodine, hydrogen peroxide, and her brother's clumsy fingers. As he worked, Phaira held out her arms and spilled out her observations:

"...razor-tipped fingers, that's got to have been noticed by someone. Dressed in all red, too; it might be a gang affiliation, or have some meaning we can trace. I got a few cuts in; didn't slow it down, I don't know why, but there must be blood on that carpet somewhere. If we can get a trace of it, maybe we can get a genetic hit."

She bit her lip, thinking. "Whoever, whatever, this assassin is, they were predictable up until tonight. But now, going after random people; the only pattern left is the method, the vicious-ness - "

"This is over our heads," Renzo interrupted.

When she glanced at him, surprised, he was looking over his glasses at her, his face pained and drawn. "Even yours."

"It's really not," Phaira reasoned. "Besides, we can't back out now. Not when something like that is out there." She gestured at her arms. "I've seen worse, believe me. You have to get used to the sight, Ren, this is part of the job."

"I don't like this," he muttered. "I don't like being responsible for healing you up."

"There's something else, Ren." She lowered her voice even more. "It disappeared."

To her delight, his response was immediate. "Cloaking?"

Phaira grinned. "Like the old stealthsuit," she confirmed. "Same shimmer, same crackle. Do you still have it?" The suit had shorted out in the Kings Canyon, weeks ago, in the middle of the great battle. She hadn't seen it since then.

"Have it?" Renzo smirked. "I'm working on applying its characteristics to the *Arazura*."

Then he went quiet, affixing white bandages to her arms. "But I think - I think we need more help," he finally admitted.

"Renzo, no."

"We need everyone we can get for this, anyone we can get who is trustworthy."

"We can't bring Sydel back," Phaira interrupted. "It's not fair. She's got her own life now. Cohen, too."

"If we told them what was happening, if we asked -"

"It's not up to us. You heard Theron. He wants to keep the circle tight."

"Since when do you listen to anyone's instructions? You can't - "

At the sound of approaching footsteps, Phaira and Renzo went quiet.

Jetsun appeared in the doorway. She had brushed out her bouffant, tied back her hair in a ponytail, and borrowed some of Phaira's clothes; in this guise, she looked young, like a college student. Her skin was also sallow, a tinge of green around her mouth.

"You need something?" Renzo was the first to break the silence. "Anti-nausea pills? You look like you're going to be sick."

Jetsun nodded. Renzo shuffled through his first-aid kit, and handed over a few plastic capsules. She swallowed them dry. Then she crossed her arms and hunched over herself.

"Start doing some research," Phaira told her older brother. "See if you can find any hits on the network on anything: the claws, the red, anything."

"And when you can talk," she said to Jetsun, "I need names of Theron's contacts, old friends, family members, anyone and everyone you can think of."

Jetsun made a face. "Why?"

Then the *Arazura* dipped a few feet, and everyone's stomach lifted, and it looked like Jetsun's was about to come out of her mouth.

"I also need a list of people he's been involved with," Phaira added.

"Why are you asking her?"

The slim white bandage was bright across Theron's dark forehead. He'd removed his jacket and rolled up his sleeves; there were bruises on his forearms, ones that Phaira tried not to look at too closely.

"Are you - willing to disclose that kind of - information?" Renzo stuttered.

Theron jerked his head at Jetsun. "More than she would be."

"Because your personal life is none of their business," Jetsun croaked.

"They're my friends," Theron said.

And no one, including Phaira, seemed to know how to respond to that.

* * *

At first, Jetsun insisted on being present at the interview, but the ship hit a patch of rough air, and she quickly retreated into Phaira's cabin. Occasionally, Phaira heard her nattering into her Lissome, giving orders, followed by the sound of moaning and retching. And Renzo was in the cockpit with CaLarca, keeping inside the clouds. Both seemed to realize that this delicate exchange of names was something to be done in private.

Phaira and Theron took their positions, sitting on either side of the common room table as if playing a game. So far, though, neither had started the conversation. She was doing her best not to fidget, running her fingers over the edge of her Lissome. He wouldn't meet her gaze. *How much is he going to reveal?* Phaira wondered, eyeing him from across the table.

Activating her Lissome, Phaira slid on her reading glasses. "So do we start with enemies, friends, or lovers?" she quipped.

"When did you get those?" He gestured at the frames.

"Recently," she said, self-conscious. "Why?"

"They're kind of adorable."

"Theron - "

"Just saying."

"We need to focus." At the same time, her thoughts were racing. How easy and familiar it was to talk to each other, even after weeks. Natural, even.

Theron leaned back in his chair. "Fine. People I know. Anandi and Emir Ajyo. Jetsun. Detective Ozias. My grandfather. Kadise."

"You know none of those are suspects," Phaira retorted. "Tell me who you've been romantically involved with."

He eyed her with suspicion.

"I don't care how many girlfriends you've had, Theron. But I suspect one of them is leaving you little bloody hearts, so stop protecting them."

"I'm not," he shot back. "I just don't believe it."

"Let's rule them out officially, then, and see if I recognize any of them."

"Yeah, that's not awkward at all," Theron muttered, crossing his arms.

"You're acting like I'm your girlfriend," Phaira said pointedly. "When I'm not."

"So what is this, then?" he asked, his index finger flicking between him and her.

"A business arrangement. Until things are resolved."

"And then what?"

She meant what she said, though, and said nothing. She had to keep things professional. Separate.

"I've only had one girlfriend," Theron finally spoke. "Gesminna Ferri. But that was years ago. She's married now, with kids."

"Did it end badly?"

"I didn't end it, if that's what you're wondering."

"No reason why she would be bearing a grudge?"

"I would be the one bearing the grudge, not her."

"So she's a cheat, then."

Theron frowned. "I didn't say that."

"It's pretty obvious, Theron. Being so vague."

"I was young," was his only response. "I learned a lot."

"Who else?" she pressed. "I have a hard time believing that she's the only one you've been involved with."

"Why?"

What kind of question is that? she wondered. Is he looking for compliments? He had to know that he was intelligent, wealthy, tall and good-looking. It was a game, it had to be a game, or some means to make her vulnerable.

After a long silence, Theron shrugged. "Well, I've had a few flings."

"How many, and how recent?"

Theron huffed. "Just in the past few months."

"Besides me," she reminded him, keeping her voice quiet, in case someone was listening.

To her surprise, his cheeks colored. "I don't call that a fling," he mumbled.

The base of her throat prickled. *If I had the courage,* she thought, strangely pleased at the revelation. *If we were in different circumstances ...*

"There were a lot of arranged dates." His words broke her reverie. "Bianco's choice. Maybe ten different women."

"Just dates?" she couldn't help but ask.

"Nothing of substance."

A very male thing to say. If he was worried about her being upset, though, he was mistaken. She'd been just as tempted for human company on her travels south, just too paranoid to take advantage. There was a difference between sex and connection. Still, there was something flattering about his careful vagueness.

A question rose in her head. "That gold gun of yours. I couldn't pull the trigger. Why?"

Theron studied her for a few seconds. Then he lifted his right hand, so the ring on his middle finger caught the light. "Sentry model," he said. "Custom-built for every Sava member. The safety only releases in proximity to the ring."

"That would have been good to know, Theron. And that you were carrying," Phaira added pointedly.

"It didn't matter, I - "

THUMP.

Theron heard it too. They both looked to the ceiling.

Then the beeping noise started.

Phaira and Theron swiveled, staring at the console that lined the common room. Every three seconds, a red light flashed. What signal was that? Phaira had never seen it before.

Then Renzo burst through, holding onto the doorframe with white knuckles.

"Breach," he panted. "There's a breach."

Phaira shoved off her chair. "Where?"

Renzo stumbled past her to the console, where he brought up the *Arazura's* schematics. There was a flashing light in one of the small storage compartments, near the front of the ship.

"But w-we're in flight," Renzo stammered. "It's not possible."

Another *thump*; this time, the sound echoed through the ventilation system.

"Get Jetsun and get downstairs. Now," Phaira ordered.

The screech of metal on metal made all three gasp.

The position had changed; the sound was coming from outside the common room.

Phaira darted over the threshold and into the corridor, staring up at the curves of the ceiling. The metal panels shuddered, one corner buckling.

Something was boring its way down.

They were trapped, in flight, in a narrow metal missile. Too many people to protect. No choice. They had to evacuate.

At the other end of the hallway, CaLarca's pale face appeared. "What's wrong? What's that beeping sound?"

"Go downstairs, activate the escape pod and get ready to jettison," Phaira ordered. "I'll send everyone down your way."

The woman's black eyes flicked to the ceiling. "Someone's in there," she confirmed. "Do you see red?"

"Not yet," Phaira said impatiently. "It doesn't matter. Do what I told you."

CaLarca's cane flashed as she made her way to the stairwell. Renzo appeared then, his arm around Jetsun, whose face was bright white with fear. Phaira directed them to follow CaLarca downstairs.

"I can't. My ship," Renzo said weakly. "I can't leave it behind."

An idea flashed in her head. "Anandi hacked into the ship's sound system and that pulse weapon remotely," Phaira recalled. "Back in Toomba. Could she do it again, and land the *Arazura?*"

"Maybe... I think so..."

"When you launch the pod, send a distress call to her, and - "

Renzo gaped at her. "You're not staying here."

"I'll be the last to board," Phaira said, glancing up at the ceiling again.

If you can get away, her mind whispered. *You know you can't defeat that thing.*

"You're not doing this alone," Theron broke in. "I'm staying, too."

In one swift motion, she had his Sentry handgun, the barrel pressed to Theron's chest. "You're not."

"What are you doing?" Renzo yelped.

But Theron didn't move, a puzzled look on his face. It was almost endearing.

"Give me the ring, and let me do my job," she told him. "Please. Go."

"Theron, come on," Jetsun pleaded, pulling at his sleeve. "It's fine, I won't tell anyone she used it."

Slowly, Theron pulled the gold ring off his finger, and dropped it into Phaira's waiting hand. It was warm, and heavier than she expected.

Then Theron turned away and descended the staircase. Jetsun and Renzo followed. When they were clear, Phaira hit the access panel. The door slid shut.

The main floor of the *Arazura* was hers.

She switched the Sentry to her left hand as she slid the ring onto her thumb, the only finger that the ring would stay on. Then she grabbed the blade from her right boot, and listened to the hiss of air from the ventilation systems; the faint clicking sounds below as the ship shifted its gears; the drip of the faucet in the tiny kitchen area. From even farther away, there was a loud roar of rushing air; the hole bored into the top of the *Arazura*, she figured, open and buckling in the wind.

The breach alarm continued to beep every three seconds.

She quieted her breath into nothing, and waited.

More sounds, like a handful of nails thrown into the ceiling above. Then a low, slow whine of metal on metal, ripping apart.

And the shadow dropped down, ten feet away from Phaira, its weight rattling the floor as it landed.

The fluorescent lights in the *Arazura* made it possible for Phaira to finally catalogue the thing's physical appearance. Human, in some form. Face hidden by a metal mask, body and head swathed in red cloth. Long arms that ended in metal-clawed fingers, already fluttering with anticipation. About her height, but a far bulkier frame, she noted. In fact, it was uneven; one shoulder was larger than the other, as was one arm. Mutated? Some kind of implants, sloppily done?

The red assassin tilted its head like an animal, its shoulders rolling slowly, one after another. Phaira had no idea who this was, what this was, or who this used to be, but it was there before her, and everyone else was below, and she had to give them time to escape.

Phaira squeezed the Sentry trigger. The sound banged through the *Arazura*, gunpowder shocking the air. A test in the light, to see if it bled or if it was made of machine.

The Red staggered back, the fabric torn in its chest, wound smoking, wetness spreading.

Then it leapt.

Phaira arched back, the whoosh of claws an inch from her throat. She spun, and took the offensive. Parrying, punching, kicking, grabbing and avoiding, lost in the blur of aggression, the quick rhythm of the dance, but aware of no voices, she realized, or even breathing from the Red. There were just strange gurgling sounds from the assassin as it caught Phaira, again and again, with the tips of those claws, her thigh, her stomach, her arm, the edge of her ear. Her own staggered breath echoed off the walls, disorienting her.

The Red slashed at her wrists, and the Sentry and blade flew away.

Then the Red had a hold of her, its claw like a cold spider latched to her forehead, pushing her backwards, pushing the back of her skull into the wall. Held in place, Phaira kicked and twisted, trying to connect with any part that might be vulnerable; straining to hold back the other metal hand that inched closer, ready to rip through her throat. But her head was being crushed in its unyielding palm, the smell of rotten breath and sharp chemicals was overwhelming, and even the metal mask was a now bloody shade of red, growing darker, as its fingertips pierced the edge of her throat....

Suddenly the Red roared and its grip loosened, just enough for Phaira to shake back her senses, slip away from its hands, and roll to the other side of the corridor. As she did, strong hands grabbed her under the arms.

Before her, the Red was buckling, snarling, trying to grab something in its back.

The hilt of her dropped knife, she realized, and Theron's hands dragging her backwards.

Despite all her training, he was still taller and stronger than her, and Phaira was too surprised to react as he tossed her down the open stairwell.

Phaira rolled, banging her head twice on the steps before catching herself. Theron stood at the top of the stairs.

Then his whole body jolted.

A choking sound erupted from his mouth.

His hands twitched over his chest.

"No!" Phaira gasped, scrambling back up the stairs.

But Theron slammed the access panel with his fist.

Phaira leapt forward and grabbed the door's edges to stop it from latching. The door shuddered in place. Her muscles screamed at her to stop. The mechanics yanked in protest. Then there was another pair of hands underneath hers, pale and tinted blue at the fingertips: CaLarca on the step below her, her teeth gritted, pulling along with Phaira. The groan of metal was horrible, and finally ended with a jerk as the access panel broke off its track, and there was just enough room for Phaira to slip through.

The copper stink of blood. Theron's body, collapsed on the floor. The Red hunched over him, a strange whine coming from its mask.

Somehow, she was on its back, and she had another knife in her hand, and she was stabbing. The Red roared and flailed, swinging her from left to right, finally gaining the momentum to grab hold of Phaira and flip her off. The knife was gone, and the Red was on top of her, straddling her, banging her skull into the floor again and again, and there was blood, and spittle, and what sounded like yelling inside of Phaira's head.

Gunfire. The shadow of the Red fell away. Through Phaira's blurry vision, she saw Jetsun with a Sentry gun, firing with one shaky arm outstretched, gripping the back of Theron's suit jacket and trying to pull him through the broken door. A flash of Renzo's blond hair and his glasses, his hands grabbing hold of Theron as well. Desperate, Phaira tried to find a foothold, tried to summon the strength to put her hand to the floor and push up, to push away. The Red was upright again. There were holes in its skin, ragged edges of what might have been skin.

Someone stood in front of her. Black boots, black leggings that shimmered in the light.

Then a cold hand wrapped around Phaira's arm, and yanked her backwards, through her own blood, through Theron's blood. Dazed, she peered up at CaLarca's sharp features, hovering above her, and saw how the woman's brow was wrinkled, how she breathed in short spurts; and how in the distance, the Red was writhing, eyes rolling and furious.

Somehow, CaLarca was holding the Red back.

Then the cold hand around her arm was gone. Phaira rolled down the last half of the stairs, landing with a gasp of pain. Pushing unsteadily to her hands and knees, Phaira felt the floor shake under her palms. A heavy path of blood led behind the training mats, where the emergency escape pod was hidden away.

The sound of a roar from upstairs.

"Go," CaLarca hissed over her shoulder, braced on the stairs, her green braids swinging.

Then Renzo's familiar face appeared, through the spots dancing in front of her eyes. Her feet kept hitting things, the air suddenly full of panic and pressure and sweat.

The accent in CaLarca's voice, telling Renzo to launch.

The ripple of fists, pounding from far away, mixed with scraping sounds, and a mighty push forward, so strong that Phaira lost her balance and hit the carpeted floor of the pod, just as the darkness enveloped her.

PART THREE

I

Under the Queline Bridge, Sydel snapped on a fresh pair of gloves, and did her best to take in a breath without actually smelling anything. Emir Ajyo glanced at her, a silent question in his eyes: *are you okay?* She gave the slightest nod before turning to her final patient, relieved that they were almost done with this scheduled stop.

"How can I help you?" she asked the man sitting in front of her.

He held up his left hand; two of his fingers were purple, wrapped in dirty gauze. Sydel placed a metal tray on her lap, drew the man's hand onto it, and ignored his yelps of pain as she straightened the broken bones.

In a way, this wasn't so different from the Jala Communia, from the ailments she treated at the clinic there: blisters, rashes, minor infections, bruises. She was secretly bored, then, and, in this moment, she was twitchy again.

Though I shouldn't be, she reasoned as she worked. This is for a charitable cause. These men and women were grateful for her attention, when the world ignored them the rest of the time. Routine boredom was sometimes part of giving back to the community; they couldn't all be incredible feats. She wouldn't want ongoing stress, anyways, not if she were to maintain her control. Not if she were to keep her affairs private, and continue to mature as a medical professional.

Under Emir's mentorship, her knowledge had certainly grown. They had become quiet companions over the past months; sharing meals, reviewing the details of the day and the schedule to come, distributing tickets and itineraries. He introduced her to colleagues; she did her best to remember their names, but there was so many faces that the names flew out of her head as soon as they came in. After all, there was only room for so much in her brain, and she studied every night in whatever room she was staying in, poring through diagrams and diagnostic studies, cramming her head to its capacity. Emir always kept a separate room, and retired early every night. He'd made enough of a recovery from the dangerous treatment for his blood disorder to function, and to help people, but his strength still wavered. Lately, he tended to sit back and let Sydel take the lead with patients, only stepping in if she made an error, and correcting gently. It was very different from her apprenticeship in Jala, where she felt so shamed, and desperate for approval.

Sometimes, she was tempted to know what Emir was thinking, what everyone was thinking, when they stared at her. But she always pushed it down. She hadn't used Eko, felt the dangerous burn of Nadi deep in her core, or felt even a hint of an Insynn rush since the day she left the Byrne family behind in Toomba. It had been weeks since she'd felt out of control of her body. Still, every day, Sydel wore gloves to prevent any accidental skin-to-skin contact, and at night, she stuffed her ears with wax, and buried herself with quilts, to blot out any possible stimulation. Just in case.

Sydel taped the man's fingers together with a splint, and gave strict instructions to keep it elevated. She could only hope that the patients would actually follow through what she asked of them; she would never see them again. That was the work she and Emir were doing, moving through the Northwest, helping where they could, and continuing on.

When the man left, Sydel gazed up at the rusty rafters of the Queline bridge, and smiled. Here she was, right where Phaira told her not to be. Would Phaira laugh, or be furious?

"Time to go," came Emir's voice from behind.

Click, snap, sweep away and dispose. Pack up the equipment and seal it away, into the storage cases they rolled into every new town. The awning was taken down, the tiny indoor space folded down and its wheels jutted out to follow behind. As usual, Emir insisted on taking the trolley, Sydel the supplies. They made their way down the street, away from the fetid stink, and Sydel was grateful for the movement, to stretch her back and legs after being hunched over for the past three hours.

In front of the doors of their Queline hostel, the shape of a small woman paced back and forth, smaller than Sydel, with copper skin and short black hair. Sydel recognized her immediately as the leader of the Hitodama hacking community, Anandi Ajyo.

"Anandi!" Emir exclaimed. His face lit up at the sight of his daughter. It was sweet.

But as they drew closer, Anandi's face wasn't joyous. It was pinched with rage.

Emir's smile dropped. "What is it?" he asked, putting down his equipment.

Anandi could only shake her head in tight little bursts, as if her anger was so intense that it could barely be contained.

"My god, Anandi, what's wrong?"

"I don't want to tell you," Anandi finally said through clenched teeth. "Because I know what you'll do."

"Now you have to tell me," Emir pointed out.

Anandi's gaze flicked to Sydel, an accusation in her blue-green eyes.

Sydel's chest grew heavy. "Phaira."

"That's part of it."

"Renzo, too?"

"And Theron Sava."

As the girl relayed the events of the past few days, Sydel tried to take in all the details. Had all of these events, murders, and injuries really taken place in the last 72 hours? (Apparently, yes.) Did Cohen know? (Anandi couldn't say, but she didn't think so.) Was Anandi able to land the *Arazura* without crashing the ship? (Yes, and the damaged transport had already been picked up and hidden away.) As Sydel listened, questions burned. Why hadn't Phaira called Sydel in to help? Sydel had long since mastered how to use the Lissome. Plus, they were friends. Isn't that what friends did?

"Do you know where they are now?" Emir queried.

"West Lea Hospital," Anandi said. "Theron was in bad shape, but he's been upgraded to stable."

"He's in a public hospital?" Emir blinked.

Anandi shook her head. "I don't think there was time for other options."

"Oh my," Sydel could only say. At the same time, she felt a flurry of excitement in her chest, instant curiosity to see what was wrong with that man. But it would be rude to inquire at this point.

"So what now?" Emir asked. "What else are they asking you to do?"

"Actually, Papa... Jetsun wants you."

"Who is Jetsun?" Sydel interrupted.

"Theron's lawyer cousin," Anandi said. "Your standard nightmare." She glanced back at her father. "She's asking me to bury the records of Theron's admission, so no one knows he got hurt. And she wants a medical professional to be there when she moves him into hiding, so she's insisting that you come to Lea."

"What about Phaira and Renzo?" Emir pressed. "Were they injured?"

"They're shaken," Anandi concluded. "But they're - "

The words burst out of Sydel. "I need to go to them."

Neither father nor daughter reacted.

"Papa, if you go," Anandi murmured, worry in her voice, "if you help him, what does that mean?"

"I don't know," Emir said. "I can't say until we get there. It's a different family now. He might be reasonable, when given kindness."

"I already said that I will go," Sydel interrupted. "I will nurse Theron Sava to health. Neither of you need to be involved."

Anandi's round face twisted. "You don't know what you're getting into."

But there was no question in Sydel's mind. "I owe him."

Anandi exhaled hard. "That's how it starts with the Savas."

"Anandi," Emir warned. "It's her decision."

His gaze softened as he turned at Sydel. "You know what he's a part of," he told her. "And you know an assassin has targeted him. That puts you in the line of fire. Are you certain that now is the time to repay your debt?"

"Yes," Sydel said. Strangely, she wasn't afraid, not at all. The idea of restoring the man to health, to protecting him from harm, it felt true, and right. "It's what I'm supposed to do."

Emir extended his hand. Grateful for his response, Sydel took it without thinking.

The world blasted white.

In the center of the light, Emir fell to his knees, grabbing at his left arm.

Then Sydel's vision sharpened, and her senses came back: the tight clasp of her fingers, the sweat on her upper lip, the fast beating of her heart.

"It's been a pleasure," Emir was saying. "Take care of yourself."

Sydel could only nod. When he released her hand, she curled it into a fist and covered it with her other fingers, as if to contain what it had just extracted.

* * *

Before she left for the southeast coast of Osha, Sydel memorized the train route, the transfer station mid-way, the route to the hospital, and Theron's room number and exact location. The journey took sixteen hours. She slept, she read about infectious disease, she meditated, she stared out of the window and ate little. It was the first time in a very long while that she had been alone. So strange, and a little frightening.

In the washroom, she stared at her reflection, and ran her hand over her short hair. It still jarred her sometimes to not feel the old heavy braids, but it was even more copper in regrowth, she noted. Her eyes were clear, her skin darker. She looked tired, but older. Closer to her own age, maybe. Maybe more formidable.

She kept her gloves on, even when they burned, even when she slept. She couldn't stop thinking about the Insynn rush with Emir. Before, when it happened with CaLarca, she had seen into the woman's past. But this felt like the future. In the hazy vision of Emir's fall, the man's beard was whiter, his body more frail. She hadn't encountered anything like it since leaving the family behind; why was it returning now?

Finally, West Lea Hospital. Her reflection in every corner of the mirrored elevator. When the doors opened to the sixth floor, the first thing she saw was green braids: CaLarca, standing guard in front of a hospital suite, her head turning in Sydel's direction.

Sydel was shocked. CaLarca was involved with this? Emotions twisted in her chest: anger, confusion, sadness.

"Sydel," CaLarca said with surprise. "You're here."

"Yes." Then Sydel didn't know what to say.

Thankfully, the door behind CaLarca opened. Phaira emerged, running a hand through her blue hair, noting CaLarca's confused expression, and turning with wide eyes to catch sight of Sydel.

For a moment, Sydel thought the woman was going to cry. There were bruises along her neck, under her eye, and scratches across her forearms and throat. Stunned, Sydel had the sudden impulse to connect via Eko and ask Phaira what was wrong. It took effort to hold herself back, to greet Phaira out loud. "Hello again."

"I didn't - I wasn't expecting you to come," Phaira stammered.

Sydel smiled. "Of course I came."

"Wait, where's Emir?" A blonde woman emerged behind Phaira; her arms crossed, her hair coiled in a messy bun.

"I'm Emir's apprentice. I'm - I'm Sydel Shovann Asanto." It was strange to say the surnames of her mother and father. She was known as just Sydel for most of her life. But now things were different.

"I'm very capable of caring for Theron Sava in place of Emir," she continued. "He was unable to come."

"You came here by yourself?" CaLarca chimed in.

"Is that a problem?" Sydel said, a little more sharply than she intended.

No one spoke. Finally the blonde woman pushed a Lissome into Sydel's hand. The medical charts, in projected, pixelated form. Relieved at the acceptance, Sydel skimmed the contents. A stab wound to the back had punctured Theron's left lung. He'd gone into hypovolemic shock from low blood pressure, oxygen drop, and blood loss. A tube had been implanted to drain the blood from his lung and expand it, intravenous fluids to treat the shock. Laceration wounds on his arms were treated, trimmed, sealed over with antibiotics. Even more interesting was his medical history: severe brain trauma as a child, resulting in seizures, migraines, disorientation, and nerve pain....

"Are you his cousin, Jetsun?" Sydel asked the woman.

The woman hesitated. "Yes. What was your name, again?"

Sydel ignored the question. "I want to speak to Theron privately."

"No," Jetsun said. "No one can be alone with him. It's dangerous."

"We're in a hospital," Sydel said. "People are everywhere."

She glanced at Phaira, looking for support, and was surprised at the yellow, agitated energy around the woman. Even CaLarca was simmering with apprehension, worry lines on her pale forehead.

They were afraid? Them?

"There's no window in there," Phaira finally spoke up, as if to reassure herself. "Ventilation units have been blocked off. This is the only way in. I won't close the door all the way, so I can hear if something... I'll be right outside. Okay?" She directed the last word at the cousin.

Jetsun deflated, muttering something under her breath, and stepped aside.

Gathering her courage, Sydel slid past CaLarca and Phaira, and walked inside the room.

Inside, the sounds of gentle beeping. The man was so tall that an expansion had been added to the bed to accommodate his length. As she came to his bedside, she saw his long black hair had been pulled back into a braid. His skin was sallow, and his cheekbones were even more pronounced. A purplish haze surrounded him, not just from the injury. Sydel looked back - the door was ajar an inch. She wet her lips and straightened her shoulders.

"Theron Sava," she whispered. "Can you hear me?"

The giant man took in a long, shaky breath, and his eyes pinched together, though they remained closed. "I know your voice." His voice was a scratchy, breathless drawl.

"Yes, we've spoken before," Sydel confirmed. "This is our first meeting in person."

Finally, his eyes opened; gold irises, red-veins in the white. "Why are you here?"

"To help you."

"How?"

"To aid in your recovery, and ensure -"

"And why would you do that?"

"Mr. Sava," Sydel said. "I know you don't like me, or want me here...."

"You're wrong." Theron took in a pained, sharp breath. "You're the only one who can help right now."

"Of course, Mr. Sava, whatever I can provide."

"I want you to heal me with Nadi."

Her mouth dropped open. She quickly shut it. "I don't know what you're talking about."

"I need to leave," he interrupted, wheezing. "Can't wait for natural healing. I know you've done it on Phaira. Do it for me now."

"No," Sydel said, stricken. "I don't do that anymore."

"You'll do as I ask," Theron commanded.

"Or what?"

Suddenly, his hot, dry hand was around her wrist. But just as quickly, his fingers went stiff. She wrestled away from his grip, too aware of the pulsing sensation in the center of her palms. Control. She tightened every nerve in her body, clenched her abdominal muscles, all the means of control that she learned from CaLarca.

Slowly, the fire faded.

"I said no," Sydel said through her teeth. "I'll sign you out, I'll supervise your recovery, but don't ask me again or you'll regret it."

Theron didn't respond. His arms lay by his sides again, hands clenched into fists. A vein protruded in his forehead.

"Syd?"

It was Phaira, peering through the doorway. Her eyes flickered to land on Theron's prone form, and then back to Sydel. "You okay?"

"It's fine," Sydel said. "We're fine."

* * *

Outside, in the hallway, everyone huddled in a circle, the conversation hushed but heated.

"We can't stay here any longer," the cousin, Jetsun, was saying.

"I'm all for moving somewhere safer," Phaira said. "Can he be moved? Is that safe?"

"That's not the only issue," Jetsun sighed. "We need muscle. We can't physically carry him and protect him at the same time. Maybe I should call one of my men."

"I'm a guy, and I'm standing right here," Renzo pointed out.

"You are shorter than me," Jetsun shot back. "What if you drop him? What if he falls?"

"Good thing that news gets around, then," came a booming voice.

Everyone turned.

Then Phaira let out a funny, girlish squeal, and then she ran, leaping into Cohen Byrne's arms. He swung her around, like they were kids, his red beard shining in the fluorescent light, his head thrown back in laughter.

"You shouldn't have come," Phaira exclaimed. Her joy shifted into fear as she grabbed her younger brother by the shoulders. "Why did you come?"

"Because you should have told me sooner," Cohen said, "when you first made this crazy arrangement. I owe the guy, too, y'know. Of course I'd come."

From behind, Sydel heard Jetsun huff: "How many people are in this family?"

Then she felt Cohen's gaze on her. His gray-green eyes were calmer than the last time she'd seen them. "Hey, Syd," he called over. "You look good."

"So do you," she admitted. And he did, healthy and strong, and strangely foreign. Perhaps he saw her in the same way. They were a long way from the days when they first met, when she was stumbling through Osha in Jala dresses, with braids wound around her head.

"Emir treating you well?"

"He's been wonderful," she confirmed. Then she added, "How is your grandmother?"

"Same as always. Stubborn and bossy. A family trait, I think." He winked at her, in that old Cohen way.

Her nerves tied up her tongue.

"If you're done catching up," came Jetsun's shrewd voice. "Inside. I need a strategy, now."

Cohen made a face at Sydel, jerking a thumb at the cousin. Delighted, Sydel held back her giggles.

Inside the hospital suite, the discussion resumed.

"Sydel, we need to know what you need to have at hand," Phaira instructed, pacing the room. "If we should bring anything along."

Or if there's something we should steal from this hospital. The thought floated through Sydel's mind. How things had changed.

"You shouldn't need anything," Jetsun said. "The *Mazarine* has a medlab inside - "

"The what?" Renzo interrupted.

"You got a rental transport waiting outside?" Cohen asked.

"No, Theron had one built," Jetsun explained. "Weeks ago. It's parked -"

"Since when?" Phaira exclaimed, a curious note of anger in her voice. "Why didn't he list it when I asked about resources? How am I -"

"Doesn't matter, Phaira," Renzo interrupted, before turning back to Jetsun. "How many people can it fit?"

"What about the *Arazura*?" Sydel asked. "I thought Anandi was able to save it. We aren't going back to it?"

"I am," Renzo said. "Can't fly it yet, there's some damage to repair, but when I'm done, we can switch back and forth."

"Wait, if you're going off to fix your ship," Jetsun interrupted, "then who will pilot the *Mazarine*?"

"I will."

CaLarca didn't react to the gaping faces, her expression as cool as ever.

"You?" Phaira sputtered.

"Since when can you fly?" Cohen demanded.

"I've learned a great deal over the past weeks. Your brother has been generous with his time and instruction."

Everyone glanced at Renzo, who raised both shoulders defensively. "What was I supposed to do? You guys leave me all alone for weeks; I needed some help. Yeah, I trained her. And yes, she should be fine as pilot. She can always call me with questions."

"Questions!" Jetsun scoffed.

"Jet." That scratchy drawl again. They all turned to the bed. Theron was awake. With visible effort, he lifted his hand. "Let her do it."

"Okay, so Ren deals with the *Arazura*," Phaira said. "And the rest of us all go - "

"Well, actually, I need Sydel to come with me," Renzo interrupted. "Just for a couple of hours. You all get Theron settled, then, CaLarca, you fly his ship to -"

"She's. The. Healer," Cohen drew out the words. "She needs to stay with the guy who's hurt."

But Renzo was unyielding. "I need Sydel," he stated. "Can't move forward without her."

"This is unbelievable!" Jetsun broke in, flinging her hands in the air. "You're splitting up? And leaving us with the same guardians as before, who have already failed in protecting their client? I should fire the lot of you!"

"Jet." Theron's voice made the woman stop short. "Enough."

Jetsun swallowed. She looked furious, but afraid too, afraid to argue with the man in the bed.

"If something happens..." she threatened Renzo.

Then she growled under her breath, waving her hand. "We get him on his ship first. When he's settled, you can leave. Send the coordinates of where you are. We pick her up in two hours, so you better finish what you need to do by then."

She pointed to CaLarca. "And you. Come with me. You'd better be telling the truth about being a pilot."

II

W hen confirmation came that the *Mazarine* was docked outside, the group moved quickly. Cohen looped Theron's arm around his shoulder and eased the giant man from his bed, while Phaira directed his long legs into the wheelchair. Then Phaira took the lead, with Cohen and Renzo flanking, and Sydel did her best to keep up, as she carried the intravenous fluids and the handheld monitor linked to his vital signs.

As they flew through the corridors, no staff spoke to them. Everyone's eyes were downturned, from the doctors to the janitorial team.

Down to the basement, to the loading docks, where a looming, dark blue ship was waiting, hatch open. As Cohen and Phaira hoisted Theron up the stairs, Renzo pushing the wheelchair behind them, Sydel realized that the interior layout was the same as the *Arazura*, with cabins on either side of a corridor, though less cluttered than the original, to be sure. She wondered what Renzo was thinking, if he was flattered or spooked.

In the meantime, she followed the group into one of the cabins, where an enormous bed took up the majority of the space, and there was barely enough room for her, Cohen and Phaira to squeeze along the mattress and half-drag, half-roll Theron into the bed. Renzo and CaLarca were already in the cockpit area, charging up the engines. Sydel felt the familiar hum of engines through the floor. Could CaLarca really fly this ship on her own?

As Cohen and Phaira left the space, Sydel did a quick scan of Theron's vitals, opening his shirt to listen to his lungs, lifting his shoulder to check the wound in his back, to ensure it hadn't broken open again. Theron glared at her the whole while. She did her best to ignore him. There was no sign of fever or infection, either, but she couldn't be gone for long, just in case. What did Renzo want with her, anyways? He refused to say out loud.

"You're fine," she announced. "Do you need pain medication to tide you over while I'm gone?"

"No. I have a request."

Sydel hit the panel on the doorframe so the door to the cabin slid shut. "I won't use Nadi on your wounds," she hissed as she turned back. "You're healing well on your own. Now that you're on board, you can rest properly and complete the process."

"You're so adamant." There was a bite in his rattling breath. "I thought you NINE took glory in your specialness."

"I'm not a NINE," Sydel corrected. "I've made a choice to be human."

"A choice," he muttered. Then, curiously, he avoided her gaze. "I want to ask you something. But I ask that it stays private."

She blinked. She couldn't imagine what he was about to say.

"I've had dreams that I can't explain."

Confused, she waited for him to continue.

"And flashes of something. When I'm awake." He took quick inhales between sentences. "At first, I thought it was just a shift. In how my seizures presented. But now is there some way to make them stop? Some kind of medication? or -"

"I don't know," Sydel said, curious. "What are you seeing when they occur?"

"The back of a skull, cut open. People begging me to change my mind." His amber eyes flicked to hers. "I saw you lying in a hospital bed, hooked up to machines."

His words shook her. Was it possible?

Yes, it made sense.Still, she could barely form the words. "You're an Insynn?"

Theron recoiled, as if stabbed. "Don't say that to me!"

"I'm sorry, but the way you reacted when you grabbed my wrist. I understand, Theron, the first time it happened to me was just as frightening."

"You're wrong," he spat. "I'm not. I'm not one of them."

He hates the NINE so much, he can't bear the thought that he might have anything in common with them.

"When did you start experiencing these flashes?"

His jaw twisted. "When the killings began."

Then he went silent for many moments. "No, not true," he finally confessed. "Longer than that. But less frequent. Not so vivid."

"Did it happen in your childhood? Can you think of any time as a child when you had a vision, when - ?"

"I have few memories," came his response. "Your NINE friends saw to that."

Growing irritated, Sydel plopped down on the mattress next to Theron, who slid back. "Why don't you tell me what happened that day in Kings Canyon," she told him. "You clearly want to."

"You don't know?"

"I know a little," Sydel admitted. "But nothing from your perspective."

His chest rose and fell. When he finally spoke, his voice was slow and flat, long breaths drawn between sentences.

"I was an only child. Other three were siblings, my cousins. Our parents took us to Kings Canyon. We ran to the edge to look down. Saw people on the canyon floor, fighting. Kuri Nimat, a red-haired girl, and two men. Kuri saw us. My mother starting walking. Tried to catch her, but she went over the edge. Then none of us could move. We could only scream. The last thing I saw was that girl, her red hair in my face. I woke in the hospital. Then I went to live with my grandfather, with my cousins."

He took in a long, wincing inhale. Sydel stared at him. It was so much more awful, this version.

Impulsively, she reached out to touch his hand. "You know, we all have a past. But we always have a choice what to do-"

He jerked it away. "You'll learn."

"But - "

A knock on the door, and Renzo's call. "Sydel? You in there? We gotta go."

When Sydel turned back to Theron, his eyes were closed.

* * *

Sydel turned Theron's story over in her head, as she followed Renzo across the train tracks, into the abandoned storage facility and rusted-over units. *What a strange man,* she thought.

What a strange situation, for all of us. I had no part in the NINE attack, but I feel responsible for so much.

The hanger doors opened with a groan. Inside, the *Arazura* caught the light, blue and glistening and perfect as she remembered, and for a moment, she was struck dumb, remembering. She had a cabin in that ship, a bed, a medical lab. For a number of weeks, it was her home. As the stairs unfurled, and Renzo entered the ship, Sydel slid her hand along the railing, listening to the quiet echo of her steps.

Inside, evidence of the attack remained in the main corridor: the smell of sweat, copper blood spattered and smeared on the floor and walls. Renzo stepped over the stains, like they were nothing, and stood underneath the hole in the ceiling. Sydel peered up as she crept closer. The metal was ripped, not cut, and inside, coils of wires hung limp.

"Is that where it came in?" she asked. "Was it hiding in the ceiling?"

Renzo grunted in response, brushing his palm down the wall, as if he caressed a loved one. "It dug its way in from the roof."

Sydel shuddered. "Can you fix it?"

"Of course I can."

"Then why am I here?"

He gestured around the splattered, broken space. "See if I missed anything before I clean up."

"Like what?"

"I don't know," Renzo said, impatience in his voice. "Whatever your brain can pick up, or your senses or energy."

"Renzo, I have abandoned that way of life."

"Sydel," Renzo interrupted her. "We're stuck. We don't know what to do, and we're all terrified, even if no one is showing it. This thing is far beyond anything we've ever seen. If you can provide any kind of insight, anything at all..."

Sydel stared at him as he talked. Was it any different from her debt to Theron Sava? Didn't she owe Renzo, and Phaira and Cohen as well? Wasn't that what friends did?

But what if, her mind railed, *what if you can't contain it? What if you hurt someone? You've come so close, so many times.*

This is different. I'll do it for them, and for only them, she decided, her body already rippling with dread.

And Sydel allowed her mind to part. It was slow to obey, like a rusted-over door, stuck in its hinges and protesting. But the world poured in, regardless, like an ocean rushing over her head. Yes, there were silhouettes brushing past her, tangling together, and voices in the walls, echoing with panic.

Sydel studied the spots on the floor. Each drop of blood had its own subtle haze of color, marking its source. The one that glowed red, that was the foreign one. She crouched down and stared at it. Her hand dropped to the floor, her fingernail grazing the edge of the stain.

Her vision turned white, then a sick, swirling vision of pink, like blood mixed with paint. She saw Phaira's face in front of her: choked, bruised, slick with sweat. Phaira's throat was in her hands, and there were clicks within her, like a clock winding. She felt a surge of strength, a rush of ice, in her veins. Her warped lips brushed against her suffocating metal mask, her jaw pushing out and back. Two syllables, released in a guttural, strangled squeal: URR-EEE-URR-EEE-URR-EEEE.

With a start, the blue-grey interior of the *Arazura* came into focus. Renzo's worried face was above her, his forehead in a series of lines, his fingers digging into her upper arms. She was being shaken.

"You're here," he was saying to her. "You're on the *Arazura*, and you're safe."

Sydel forced herself to blink and breathe. That horrible screeching sound echoed in her head. She flexed her fingers; it felt like breaking through a frost.

"Show me," she managed.

"What?" Renzo demanded. "Show you what?"

She reached out, gesturing for him to pull her up. He did, reluctantly, eyeing her over his glasses. She put a hand to her chest, feeling for her heartbeat. It was present, and racing.

"Show me the path it took," she finally spoke. "From start to finish."

Renzo grumbled, but he still brought her to the top of the *Arazura*, to the gaping hole in the roof, where the assassin broke in. Sydel lowered herself down into the darkness, and followed the energetic path of the assassin, crawling and shimmying through ventilation shafts, attacked by vision after vision. The click of metal on metal; the sound of voices, wafting through the pipes; the fainter sound of an alarm, relentlessly beeping; more internal clicks, more shots of cold rushing through her body.

Finally, she reached the hole in the inner corridor, and looked over the edge. All the wreckage and bloodstains below, back where she started. Carefully, she lowered herself through, stepping onto the ladder Renzo held below, her mind whirring with all the new images.

"Are you seeing things?" Renzo asked.

Sydel made her way to the floor, and turned to face the entryway to the lower floor, where blood streaked all the way down the stairs. "You all managed to get to an escape pod."

She noted the claw marks of where it gripped the walls, and the dried drops of red. Sydel closed her eyes and let the memory take over. Flashes of light. The sound of screeching air. Her ears popping, the sudden jostle of metal on earth. Then, bright sunlight, and grasslands stretching in all directions. In front of her, the sun burned and burned, and stayed in sight, even as the horizon dragged and eventually faded.

"Where did Anandi land the *Arazura*?" Sydel asked, coming back to the present.

"Halfway between Lea and the Mac, in an empty clearing. Why?"

"When it disembarked, the assailant went in the direction of the sun," she reported, wiping her hands on her trousers, as if to remove the stain of the visions.

Renzo brought up his Lissome. The translucent screen projected between them, showing the map of the East Coast of Osha; a red dot indicated where the *Arazura* was found. Sydel studied the ripples of mountains and valleys to the west. There, within ten kilometers, a small town: Cardine. When Renzo checked the local registry, there were three listed doctors and a public transit station.

"Any recent reports of violence there?" Sydel asked. "Thievery? Suspicious behavior?"

Renzo smirked, his fingers fluttering over his Lissome. "You sound like Phaira." There was a beep, and Renzo frowned. "Nothing on record."

She hesitated, then, with her impulse, uncertain if she really meant it. Yes, she did. "I could go there, and investigate."

Renzo recoiled. "What? By yourself?"

"That assassin hasn't seen my face." A second thought occurred to her. "Nor Cohen's. We can be your eyes. Go to Cardine and see if any clues are there."

Renzo shook his head, again and again.

Sydel sighed, and put her hand on his cheek to stop the motion. "Renzo," she said firmly. "We must do something. You are all stuck in place. I'm not. And if Cohen is willing…"

Renzo's jaw dropped. "I can't believe I'm hearing this from you."

"I'm just as determined as the rest of you to learn what this is all about," Sydel said, lowering her hand. "And who this Red person is, and how to stop this bloodshed."

* * *

Sydel left a shaken Renzo to his repair work, and trekked through the warehouses, moving to the property edge, where CaLarca was slated to meet her with the *Mazarine*. As she walked, she tried to focus, and decipher the strange noises she heard. There was a clue there, she knew it, if only she could recover it...

A shadow in the distance. Sydel stiffened. Then she recognized the slim silhouette, and the face under the wide-brimmed black hat.

"You done?" Jetsun Sava called over as she scanned the sky.

"Yes," Sydel said. She shielded her eyes from the sun and stood next to the woman. Her heart skittered. More than anything, she wanted to slump down to the ground, close her eyes, and block out the images rotating in her head.

"Anything new to share?"

"A path to follow," Sydel said cautiously. "Perhaps. And you? Why are you here?"

"Just had to take care of a few things on land. The sooner I get onboard, update Theron and get off, the better." She tipped her head up, so her eyes were visible under her hat. "I have to ask: are you really the long-lost daughter of Joran Asanto?"

Sydel stared at the concrete ground. "So I've been told."

"You've never laid claim to the family estate."

"I only learned of my heritage recently."

"You registered as Sydel Shovann Asanto to medically clear Theron. Is that the first step?"

"I haven't decided yet," Sydel shot back.

"If you need some help navigating the legal waters," Jetsun said smoothly, "I can be of service."

"For a price, I'm sure."

Jetsun's lips were red, grinning without teeth. "You'll have plenty to spare, if you're the true thing."

"I don't care about money," Sydel said.

"You say that now," Jetsun said, "but you'll find something to do with it, I'm sure." She quirked her blonde eyebrow at Sydel.

"It'll be a fight, though. I'm familiar with the estate. You could use someone who knows the soft spots."

For whatever reason, the term 'soft spots' made Sydel think of Kuri, and his manipulations, and his desire for her blood and her signature, all in the name of gaining access to the Asanto fortune.

"If someone wished to make a claim," she blurted out, "could someone just use my blood and a signature, to gain access on my behalf?"

"No," Jetsun said, her voice serious for the first time. "Of course not. The blood withdraw must be witnessed, the results notarized. And a signature isn't worth a thing. There's paperwork, official rulings, not to mention court fees if the claim is contested. You can't just show up with a vial and expect a bag of rana. What gives you that idea?"

"It wasn't my idea," Sydel muttered. "But is it really so complicated? To take a surname?"

"Everything that involves rana is complicated," Jetsun said. "But if you're legitimate, then it's legally yours. Just depends if you have the courage to go for it."

Was the woman trying to prod Sydel into action? Sydel narrowed her eyes. "You're a mob lawyer, for murderers and thieves."

"I'm a licensed attorney, with a powerful family," Jetsun corrected. "I'm not exclusively evil, thanks. I abide by the rules."

"The rules that you can slip past, I'm sure."

Jetsun waved her hand dismissively. "Oh, please. Listen: prove you are who you are first, and I'll ensure you get what you're entitled to, no matter who opposes - "

There was a rush of wind, and the sun was blocked out. Both women looked up, into the silhouette of the ship, descending from above.

"Time to finish this," Sydel heard the other woman mutter, over the rush of wind and engines, before swallowing a handful of pills: anti-nausea, by the smell.

Do I have other family?

Since the revelation from CaLarca, Sydel had been afraid to look deeper into any blood connections, choosing to bury herself in her work with Emir. Now, blank faces swarmed in her mind as she watched Cohen take Jetsun by the wrist and hoist her onto the rope ladder.

When Jetsun disappeared into the darkness, Cohen gestured for Sydel to follow.

She shook her head. Then she patted at her hips, making her hand into a gun and lifting her eyebrow, inquiring.

Holding onto the frame of the entryway, Cohen showed her his firearm, locked at his waist.

She nodded, and gestured for him to come down.

Cohen glanced back. Then he vaulted off the platform. Landing with a *thunk!* dust billowed around his feet.

"Are you okay?" he yelled, over the rumble of the engines.

She nodded again, noting the shape of his Lissome in his pocket. Sydel removed it, twisted it in two, and placed the adhesive square under her ear, wincing only a little at the automated pinch.

"It's Sydel. I'm taking Cohen," she announced. "Fly off, and don't ask."

There was no response from inside. But the *Mazarine* ascended into the sky, picking up speed.

Soon the wind died down, and everything was silent. Sydel removed the Lissome from her ear, and joined it with its other half. Then she tried out a smile on Cohen, who was staring at her with confusion.

"I have a lead," Sydel said shyly. "We're the only ones who can move unnoticed, I think, to follow it."

Cohen looked back up at the clouds. Then he shrugged. "Okay."

Sydel smiled at him. "Finally alone."

"I know." He shuffled his feet. "So - can I - ?"

"Yes."

He smelled of grass, and the woods.

Then his hands were on her face, and she stood on the balls of her feet, the scruff of his beard a strange, but appealing sensation as he kissed her.

III

After a bus ride out of Lea, they were finally on the train to Cardine. Sydel removed her shoes and crossed her legs on the seat. Her hip strained a little at the angle, but she ignored it, rubbing her cold, bare toes, and arching her back, feeling the tiny pops in her spine. She took in a long, cool breath of air, and folded her hands together, her fingers entwined, her thumbs touching, and tried to relax.

Cardine would be the key, she knew it. They would find something to tell them where that assassin was next. Of course it was very possible that the red threat was following them right now. Or it was tracking down Theron and the others. She tried not to think about those scenarios too much. Now that her Eko was active again, she felt certain that she could pick up on any hostility.

And Cohen was more imposing than ever. Sitting across the aisle on the train, his legs splayed, he looked fierce and determined. Then he leaned over the armrest in her direction.

"It's great to be here with you. Finally." There was a tiny exhalation at the end of it, like he couldn't believe what was happening. "Wish it was under better circumstances."

"I know," Sydel said. Instinctively, she reached across the aisle and took his hand.

He squeezed her fingers. "Surprised Emir let you go. You guys had so many stops still to make."

"He understood," Sydel said. "Was it difficult to leave your grandmother? Vyoma was ill," she recalled their last conversation. "A mini-stroke, you said, only a couple of weeks ago."

"She's doing much better. Back to bossing around the militia. She says hello, by the way."

That, Sydel didn't believe. Vyoma never liked Sydel, or CaLarca for that matter; she was always suspicious, and for good reason, given CaLarca's deception.

But then again, Cohen swore that Vyoma was the reason behind his first call via Lissome, the first time they spoke after separating, just two weeks into her travels with Emir. She was stunned to hear from him, since they had left on such strange terms.

When the line connected, Cohen didn't waste any time. "I've been thinking about things, and I wondered if maybe I ruined everything."

"You didn't ruin anything," Sydel said haltingly, heat rushing to her face. "I was a mess. We were all in a mess. It's better that we all separated and -"

"I just thought - y'know, Syd, things happen that we can't predict. And it's best to be honest."

Honesty. She closed her eyes. Yes, honesty. "What is it you want to know, Cohen?"

"Are we... friends?"

"Of course we are. Though," she added, flushing from head to toe. "I don't know if the term is... satisfactory."

He was silent for a long time after that. Finally, he spoke. "Did you - back in Jala Communia - did you ever have a boyfriend?"

"No," Sydel said timidly, wondering if that made her lesser in his eyes.

He stumbled over the next words: "Would you be open to having one?"

Smiling to herself, Sydel came back to the present: the rumbling train, the heat pressing through the windows, his hand dropping from hers, already damp with sweat.

"Cohen," she murmured. "I'm thinking about going public. About who I am."

He glanced over his shoulder. "When?"

"Soon. I spoke to Theron's cousin, that lawyer."

"You can't trust what she says, Syd."

"Maybe. But I've wanted to know who I am for years. Now that I know, why hesitate to claim what's rightfully mine?" Sydel gave a firm nod at her statement. "You know, I would be a good wealthy person," she declared. "Honest. Charitable. Working hard to help people."

Cohen laughed. "See that? You know who you are, Syd. A name isn't going to change that."

"When we find this assassin, when this is done, will you come with me to file the motion?"

Cohen's grin faded. Sydel shook her head at him. "Don't start worrying."

"I'm always gonna worry. How many times does it seem like things are getting better, then they're not?"

Poor man. He was right. But this time would be different, she would make certain. Sydel took Cohen's hand again and kissed the back. "This part is good," she reassured him. "This is the part that's good."

"You know, Syd, it's only been a few months," Cohen said, gazing at her, "but you're different. I can see it. More confident. More sure of yourself."

"I see the same in you. Toomba has been good for you, I think."

"It's been an education." He narrowed his eyes as the train slowed, and the edges of Cardine came into focus.

"When we get in there," he said under his breath. "Whatever it takes, Syd, you know that, right?"

"I know," Sydel said. Her stomach was warming, like coals smoldering. "I'm ready."

"Damn right you are. Let's find this thing."

* * *

Sydel held Cohen's arm as they wound through the shabby streets of Cardine, getting their bearings of the town's layout. No one paid much notice; those who did even gave them a smile. It helped that they presented as a couple. As they walked, Sydel relayed all she had seen in the *Arazura*.

"The Red would need a medical professional," Sydel concluded. "A skilled pair of hands, to reach all the stab wounds in the back, and seal them properly."

"Couldn't they just bandage it?"

Sydel shook her head. "I felt the wounds, their width and depth. They wouldn't stop bleeding on their own. The Red might be able to manage the blood flow but within the day, they would need to be sealed to prevent infection."

"Well, there're only three doctors listed in this town," Cohen said, looking at the crowds before them. "I guess there could be people unlisted, though, in the underground." He sighed. "This is going to be tough. What do we do first? Where do we look?"

"I know Theron said not to involve Anandi," Sydel said, "but she can check cameras and surveillance, and give us a direction to go in. It seems foolish to not use her skills."

"If he wants our help," Cohen concluded, "he's got to open up. And she's discreet. At least I think she is."

"She's a good person," Sydel said. "I think she would want to stop a killer from hurting anyone else."

Cohen grinned down at her. "Logical, as always."

Ducking into a alleyway, he activated his Lissome and punched in the cc. It rang three times before Anandi's voice, tinny and angry, came through the sound system. "I'm not being dragged into this, so don't ask."

Cohen frowned. "We're just asking you to access some -"

"No. I don't care what Theron's gotten himself into. It's his own damn fault."

Sydel stared at the Lissome. "Why do you hate him so much?"

"You don't know that family like I do. Once you do one favor, it never stops, and then you're sucked into doing things you never...." Anandi's voice trailed off.

After a few moments, she spoke again, quieter now. "I heard rumors that he's in a bad way."

"He's stable," Sydel said. "And safe, for the time being."

The girl's bitter tone returned. "Too bad. If he had died, then the Savas could have torn themselves apart on their own. Now they will hold steady until something changes. Either Theron dies, or he's victorious."

"This is more than Theron," Cohen cut in. "This goes beyond whatever problem you've got with him. That Red thing killed bodyguards, sure, but it also killed two people and spilled their guts everywhere. It almost killed Phaira, wrecked the Arazura, and it's still out there, still dangerous, still angry, still after Theron and the people around him. That's us, Anandi. Doesn't that matter to you?"

"You're shaming me into doing this?"

"Yeah, I am," Cohen snapped. "You're supposed to be a friend, and friends help friends to not get murdered."

The line was quiet for many, many seconds.

"You tell no one," came her voice finally. "You found the information on your own."

"I think people will have a hard time believing that," Sydel said.

"I don't care. Make up a story. My name never gets mentioned. I'll deny it if you say I did, to anyone, and that includes Renzo and Phaira."

"Fine," Cohen said, before Sydel could protest further. "Find out if there's been any Cardine arrests or warrants in the past two days. Could show up as vandalism or assault, stealing medical supplies, car-jacking...."

"Way ahead of you," Anandi said. "The Cardine East Bay Clinic reported minor vandalism two days ago, and shut down. Still closed, by their accounts, for repairs. Also, five reports of stolen vehicles in the past forty-eight hours; guess they have a problem with that around here..."

"Surveillance footage of the clinic?" Sydel asked.

"None that documents the vandalism; it was disconnected for a few hours, and when it went back online, the place was already closed."

"That's it," Cohen said. "That's got to be it. That wasn't so hard, wasn't it?"

"Don't joke," came Anandi's low response. "And don't call me again. Got it?"

And the Lissome disconnected.

* * *

Standing on tiptoe, Sydel tried to peer through the clinic windows, but they were covered in paper. "Should we break in?" she asked over her shoulder, at Cohen.

Cohen chortled. "I can't believe you just said that."

"Why isn't there anyone in there, cleaning up, or making repairs?" Sydel wondered. "If it were just some act of vandalism, they would be trying to get it back to operational as soon as possible. But it's just closed, and empty."

Cohen's smile dropped. "What if the Red is still in there? Hiding out?"

"It's not in there."

"Are you sure?"

When Sydel gave him a look, he lifted his hands. "Okay, sorry, I forgot who I'm talking to here." He looked up, noting the position of the sun. "Go in after dark?"

Sydel stared at the clinic's door. "Do we really have time to wait?"

"I don't want to get arrested breaking into a place while carrying a firearm, Syd," Cohen pointed out. "You'll see me again in twenty years."

Sydel bit her lip. "I don't think we can wait. I think we need to get in there, now, and get what we need."

"Which is what?"

"I'm not sure yet."

Cohen sighed. Then he bashed his wrapped fist into the window frame, cracking the glass. Sydel kept watch for any patrol, half-wondering what she might do if someone were to emerge, as Cohen dismantled the rest of the glass, and helped her to climb inside.

Their feet sank into dark green carpet. Surprisingly, despite the report, there wasn't any visible damage in the waiting room of the clinic: ugly peach paintings, and worn furniture, but no wreckage. Why was it closed, then? Light filtered through the papered windows, streaks of sun showing all the dust in the air.

Moving as quietly as they could, Cohen and Sydel crept through the double doors, passing rows of empty cots.

There was an office at the back, the lights on inside. Slowing his pace, Cohen held out an arm, keeping Sydel behind him as he reached for his firearm and primed it with his thumb.

When Cohen pushed the door open, the stench of bleach hit Sydel so hard it made her dizzy. There was a yelp: a man crouched on the floor, scrambling back with a sponge in hand. "You shouldn't be here!" he gasped, coughing and holding his ribs. "We are closed, can't you read the signs? This is trespassing!"

Bruised ribs, Sydel thought. *Maybe even broken.* Her attention went to the far corner, to a crumpled tissue; garbage in any other's view, but she was drawn to it, somehow.

"Someone hurt you?" Cohen demanded.

The man shrank away. "No. There was an accident. Some kids spilled some chemicals, and we had to close. Look, I'll alert patrol if you don't remove yourself from the property."

"That what you're cleaning up?" Cohen asked, gesturing at the floor. "Two days later?"

The man's eyes were wide with fear. "Please. I won't tell anyone you were here."

Sydel brushed past Cohen. The man flinched. "Please," he begged. "I can't - I can't - "

Ignoring his pleas, she walked past him to the corner, and crouched down to scoop up the tissue in her hands. As she straightened, the man tried to grab it from her.

"Hands off!' Cohen snarled.

The man recoiled, and Sydel unfurled the tissue carefully.

Wrapped inside was a piece of metal, no bigger than a piece of rice.

"What is this?" Sydel asked the doctor.

"Nothing. It broke off one of my tools."

Sydel held the piece of metal between her thumb and index finger. It was dull, but compact and unmarked. And it pulsed, like a tiny heartbeat, framed in red energy.

With a burst, the man bolted for the exit. Cohen blocked the way.

"The person in red came to you for medical treatment," Sydel said slowly. "Puncture wounds in the back, correct?" She held up the metal piece. "Did this come from its body?"

"I can't say!"

"Tell us what you know," Sydel demanded.

"I won't."

"You will, or I will take it out of you." The words left her mouth before she had a chance to think about it.

Cohen was staring at her, his face in shadow, but his shock still identifiable.

"Whatever is necessary," she reminded him.

Cohen swallowed, and took the trembling man by the shoulders, turning him to face Sydel.

"Please," the man whispered to her. "Please just let me go."

"Then tell us what we need to know," Sydel insisted.

When the man shook his head again, something inside of her twisted and let go. Her motions were automatic. One hand resting on the man's head, the other hand before his face, thumbnail extended, drawing a vertical line down the span of his forehead.

The man's world spilled through. Sydel kept to the edges of the gossamer threads, the most vibrant, the most recent, and coaxed them into view. There it was: the doctor in this very office, working late, startled by a noise; the sound of metal on tile, a strange, screeching whine. Then the flood of red: red clothes, red blood; the pressure of a cold, clawed hand on either side of his throat, squeezing out the air; hot, sour breath, so close she could see the condensation on the intricate metal mask the creature wore, and the Red's eyes through the openings: blood crusted over one eyebrow, the other one bloodshot and wild.

The Red unwound yards of dirty, red fabric from its body, revealing a pale back, grotesque muscles, knobby spine and discolorations, and the patchwork job over its stab wounds, already bleeding through the dirty gauze.

"Fix it," came a guttural voice.

Shaking, the doctor did as demanded, suturing the punctures. Sydel listened to his terrified observations: the Red was missing half its left ear; tattooed with some strange pattern along its lower ribs; its breathing was artificial, running through some kind of mechanical system...

When the doctor finished stitching the wounds, the Red wound the fabric around its body again. As it did, Sydel felt the sensation of fingertips, reaching underneath the counter, groping for something, finding a button, and pushing it until it was flush against the wood. The doctor's panic button.

The Red heard it. The backhand sent the doctor flying into his desk. Amidst the pain, she heard the sound of skittering feet, hissing noises.

Sydel closed the Eko gap. The doctor slumped to the ground.

"Did you find it?" Cohen asked her. "Should I call for a pick-up?"

Staring at the doctor on the floor, Sydel gripped the tiny piece of metal so tight that it pierced the skin of her palm. The doctor's eyes were open, but his breath was shallow, and his body jerked every few seconds.

Tears filled her eyes. She grabbed Cohen's hand and pulled him. "Go. Now. I need to go."

They climbed back through the window, and once they hit the ground, they both broke into a run, flying down alleys and between buildings, hands clasped the entire while. When she couldn't breathe any more, Sydel stopped and slumped against a brick wall. Cohen had said nothing, only followed where she led. Now, as she gripped her hands into fists, he was trying to catch her eye. "Syd."

Shame flooded through her. "Please don't tell the others what I did."

"Oh, Syd," Cohen sighed, rubbing the back of his shaved head.

Her eyes spilled over with tears. "I've never done that when the person wasn't willing."

"This was an emergency," Cohen reasoned. "What did you see?"

"The Red's body. Tattoo on the lower back. Artificial breathing mechanism. It's enhanced artificially in some way."

"See? That's fantastic! That makes it worth it, Syd."

But she shuddered at the memory of what she'd done. "I was tempted to keep going. To keep pushing further."

"But you didn't," Cohen broke in. "You stayed on the surface, and got what we needed. I'm sure Renzo can create some kind of program and find the Red now, and we can stop this thing from killing again."

She kept her eyes fixed on the ground, as Cohen spoke into his Lissome, asking for a pick-up.

But her thoughts were on a loop: *I t's what Huma did to Phaira.*

The same thing. I did the same invasive Eko.

I couldn't stop myself.

IV

On the outskirts of Cardine, the *Mazarine* eased down its landing gear without a sound. When the hatch opened, no one was there to greet them. Wary, Sydel went first, creeping inside the oddly-familiar interior, searching for signs of life. The corridor was silent, every door closed.

So she headed for the cockpit. There was CaLarca, at the controls.

"Any changes?" she asked the green-haired woman.

"Everyone has been quiet. Save for Jetsun. She was sick again." CaLarca rolled her eyes. "Had to drop her back on the ground almost as soon as she got on board."

"And Theron?"

"No change. See for yourself."

In the narrow space between bed and wall, Phaira stood guard next to Theron. When she turned at the sound of entry, Sydel frowned; Phaira's eyes were dull, and there was a waxy sheen to her skin.

"Well?" Phaira broke the silence. "What did you two find?"

"This," Sydel said. She removed the tissue from her pocket, and held up the metal splinter.

Everyone leaned forward to peer at it.

Then Theron jerked, half-sitting up. "Where did you get that?" he demanded.

"You know what this is?" Sydel asked, surprised.

Theron's face had changed from ashen to red. "You went to my apartment. You went through my belongings." He glared up at Phaira. "Did you know they were doing this?"

"Hold on!" Cohen exclaimed. "We were in Cardine, not Lea. Why, what is this thing, you recognize it?"

Theron struggled to brace himself against his pillows. "I need to speak to Sydel alone," he wheezed.

"Why?" There was a challenge in Phaira's voice, and they all heard it.

"I'm not arguing with you," he rasped. "Please."

Phaira's mouth twitched, like a thousand words were bottled up against her lips, but she ducked out of the room before Sydel could say anything more.

Cohen sighed loudly. He was already growing tired of secrecy, Sydel noted, they all were. She had to get Theron to talk, to trust her, if they were going to come out of this.

By the time the door closed, and they were alone, Theron had managed to sit up fully. He looked more vulnerable, somehow, as he held out his hand. "Can I see it?" he wheezed.

She tipped her palm, and let the metal piece fall. He brought it to his eyeline, studying it.

Then, to her surprise, he laughed to himself.

"What is funny?"

"Not what I thought it was," he was muttering. "I'm so stupid."

"And what did you think it was?"

"If I had just kept my mouth shut." His smirk faded, and he hit his fist on his thigh.

"Stop hiding from us," she told him. "If you know who this person is -"

"Sydel," he interrupted. "Before this goes any further. Please heal me with Nadi."

"I won't."

"Your debt to me will be paid."

She faltered at that. Would it?

"If you do it and it works, I'll leave," he continued, taking short breaths between sentences. "Never hear from me again. None of you will. Don't need to be involved with this. You don't want to be. None of you do. Just tell them I threatened you. Make me the villain. They'll be glad to cast me off."

Sydel didn't know what to say. But the longer she stood there, the more acceptable it sounded. They had done so much for him already. She could provide him with the clues she uncovered, and if he was healed, he could pursue the Red on his own. Phaira, Cohen and Renzo would be out of danger. She could be absolved, finally, of her debt to his family, for what had been done to him in Kings. Even CaLarca could finally be sent away. Perhaps this was why she was supposed to come back: not to stop a killer, but to protect her friends.

She couldn't help but blurt out: "You seem ill-suited to the position you are in."

That smirk of his returned. "A lot of people agree with you."

"Tell me what you thought that piece of metal to be."

"And then?"

Sydel swallowed. "Then I will try to help you -"

"I found an implant," came his breathless response, his cold tone back in place. "In the back of Kuri Nimat's skull. This piece looks similar to that. But it's not."

"What?" Sydel exclaimed.

But Theron pulled his shirt over his head, exposing his broad back to her. "We made a deal," he reminded her.

But Sydel's hands felt heavy as lead, and just as cold. "Is Kuri still alive?" she managed. "Did you recover his body?"

"Hurry," he hissed.

Sydel stared at the curve of his spine. "Tell me what you did with Kuri."

Theron swiveled at the waist, wincing as he did so. "I made a trade with the Toomba militia. I took him. I found that sliver of metal in his skull. When he was eventually dead."

"You killed him? Why did you do that?" Sydel demanded.

"You cast your vote to have him picked clean by the birds in the mountains." he spat. "Does it matter he lived a few days longer?"

He wasn't wrong. It was no different, she realized with a sinking stomach.

Still, something was pinging, deep inside her. Kuri. Kuri. What if... what if....

"The Red wants revenge," she listed slowly. "It has artificial enhancements. And suspected NINE abilities. When it was fighting with Phaira, I think - "

She pushed out the words. "I think it might have been saying the name 'Kuri' again and again."

Theron's anger fell from his face.

"He's dead," he stated, though his dark eyebrows were knit together. "He's been dead for weeks."

"What if he's not, somehow?"

"Not possible. His body is where I left it."

"Do you know that for certain?"

Theron's mouth opened and closed, but even as he shook his head, she could see the dread in his eyes. "No technology to support that," he offered weakly. "Re-animation doesn't exist."

"Who is to say what exists?" Sydel countered. "Look at all we've seen in the past months. Where is his body?"

Theron stared at her. Then he drew out his Lissome and spoke a series of letters and numbers.

"Theron?" came Jetsun's voice. "What's wrong?"

"Confirm something for me," he coughed.

"Of course, anything. I'm back with Renzo and the *Arazura's* finished now, so we -"

"Confirm that Kuri Nimat's body is where I left it."

There was a long pause.

"What did he say?" Sydel heard Renzo's yelp through the speakers.

But Theron clicked the Lissome closed, turning away from Sydel.

"Quickly," he muttered over his shoulder. "Do it."

Sydel took in a deep breath, studying his back on her exhale. Then she let the planes of her vision shift, and she saw the blood flowing through his veins, the ripple of his heartbeat, the electrical flutters of his brain. She saw the pink of his injuries, the strangled puff of his lungs, and the clusters of threads, red blood, black scarring, dancing and weaving.

When she put her hands on him, Sydel felt the floor beneath her shudder.

The fire billowed inside her, through her arteries and the bones of her arm, into her palms and fingertips. She focused on the threads, gathering them, pulling them away from the red. Theron made strangled noises of pain as she pulled the threads taunt, binding the muscle, fusing the cells; coaxing the lungs to expand.

The floor dropped away. Sydel's stomach lurched into her throat. Theron's back floated before her for an instant, before settling.

Something was wrong. She had to finish.

With a burst of energy, she drew together the final edges of Theron's wounds. Scars from the puncture wounds were left, of course, but sealed over, and lungs repaired. It was done. His breath wasn't strained any longer. She had done it. They were even. He could breathe, and so could she.

And Phaira was in the doorway, she realized; one hand on either side of the frame, as if to hold herself up.

Her eyes darted from Sydel, who was covered in sweat, to Theron, hunched over on the bed.

"We're hitting turbulence," Phaira finally spoke. "We need to strap down."

The ship rocked violently. Phaira grabbed Sydel by the forearm and hauled her into the corridor, to the open jump seat just outside the door. "Get in there," she ordered. "I'll get him secured."

Shivering, and woozy, Sydel buckled the black straps over her chest, and craned her neck over her shoulder to look into

Theron's cabin. To her shock, there was a fight going on. In the far corner of Theron's cabin, a jump-seat had unfolded – only one - but the newly-healed Theron was already there, and yanking Phaira by the waist onto his lap. She was wrestling away from his grip, but he paid no heed, pulling the straps of the harness over them both and fastening just in time, as the *Mazarine* plummeted, dropping one hundred feet. Sydel shrieked.

"Syd! You okay?" Cohen's panicked voice came over the intercom.

She tried to say yes, but her throat was choked with fear.

Another drop, and shudder. Sydel gripped the straps that bound her and shut her eyes. *Catch it. Catch it,* she pleaded in her head.

Another jostle. Then another, but less violent.

The shaking gradually turned into a constant shudder. CaLarca had regained control of the flight, it seemed.

Worried, Sydel glanced back into Theron's cabin. Were they safe?

Yes, Phaira and Theron were still locked in. One of Theron's hands clasped her thigh; the other was around her waist, his forehead in her shoulder. And Phaira was gripping the back of both his hands with hers, their fingers on the cusp of being interlaced. Sydel could see their chests rising and falling in unison.

It was strangely, almost embarrassingly, intimate.

They're involved, Sydel realized.

V.

W hen the turbulence finally eased into stillness, no one
spoke. Everyone on board Theron's ship averted their
eyes, and went in different directions, closing doors to cabins
and to cockpits, like too much was revealed; too many fears
were out in the open, needing to be reeled back in. Sydel spent
the rest of the afternoon in the cabin she shared with CaLarca,
scrolling through information on the Asanto estate on her
Lissome.

As she did, her mind wandered. Phaira, and Theron Sava.
It made sense, somehow. For how long, though? And to what
extent? Had anyone else guessed at their relationship?

She forced herself to concentrate and read. The official
death notice, from twenty years ago, said that Joran Asanto and
his wife Tehmi Shovann died while hiking in Kings Canyons,
both falling from an unsteady rock path. No mention of a preg-
nancy, nor child. Joran had left his rana to the foundation in his
name, and now the Asanto Foundation was one of the foremost
givers in Osha. But while the Foundation was visible, the ones
who made the funding decisions were not. In fact, the trustees
had remained anonymous since the foundation's start. A few
curious articles had been written about the Foundation, its secrecy and generosity; the general consensus was that as long
as they were a fiscally responsible organization, no one much
cared who controlled that money. And so it remained, for the
past twenty years. The only spokesperson who ever appeared

was an unidentified man, who refused photographs and left quickly after presentations....

It was too much to take in. She needed to walk, to breathe, to speak to someone about what she had found.

When Sydel entered the hallway, she heard whispers. A door was ajar. Sydel eased next to the opening, concentrating on the barely-audible voices within.

"....enough running," Phaira was saying. "You held your own against me, when we sparred back at your house on the cliffs. And those men who came into the apartment in Liera, if they hadn't self-identified, you could have killed them. You have leagues of men at your command. More money than most in Osha. You're far from helpless, Theron. But you're acting like if you just ignore it, it will eventually go away. It's not going away."

She was in there with Theron? He wasn't saying anything, though. What was he thinking? What was Phaira thinking?

"Come with me."

Sydel blinked at the urgency in Phaira's voice.

"Meaning what, exactly?" Theron retorted.

"I'm not waiting around for it to attack me, or anyone else, and neither should you, now that you're healed up. Sydel and Cohen found the Red's path. Let's continue it on our own. And find whomever is helping it. Like that metal piece, or its cybernetic enhancement, there's got to be something to trace."

"You want to leave them behind?"

"It's after you, not them, remember? And Jetsun and Renzo are surrounded by patrol and Sava surveillance, you know that as well as I do."

Theron snorted a little, but he didn't argue the point.

Is that true? Sydel wondered. *What else is being hidden from us all?*

"Use your connections," Phaira continued. "If you wanted cybernetic enhancement, where would you go? Have you heard of it before this incident?"

"Not much," he admitted.

"Not much is more than I have," Phaira said. "Where have you heard of it?"

"Just rumors, within the syndicate."

"So let's go digging," Phaira said.

"You're willing to do that?"

"This was my idea, remember?"

A long pause. Sydel glanced back at the cockpit. She wondered if she should sneak away, or make her presence known.

"You need to sleep first, Phaira."

"I'll sleep when -"

"I mean it. No more injections." Theron's voice was gentler than she'd ever heard.

Of course. Phaira had been using REM injections since the incident on the *Arazura*. The benefit of a few hours of sleep in ten minutes, designed for one-time use by long-term travelers or on military missions. Sydel had seen several injector addicts, working with Emir in the north. And Phaira had the same look as many of them: the smudge of muddy-purple under each eye, the unnatural sheen to her skin. Why hadn't Sydel realized it before?

"You do that," Theron continued. "I'll determine where we are in the trajectory, and where the ideal place is to drop."

Sydel heard Phaira exhale. "Fine. But don't go without me. I mean it. I'll find you if you do."

Theron didn't say anything, but his thoughts were strong enough to float through Sydel's mind.

You always do.

* * *

A shrill alarm jarred Sydel from sleep. She had slumped over, against the wall of her shared bunk, asleep without even knowing it.

As Sydel ran into the corridor, she caught sight of CaLarca, braced at the entrance to the cockpit. "What is that? Another breach?" the woman cried out.

Sydel reached out with her mind, searching for bodies and minds on board. There should be five, but two were moving farther and farther away.

She ran into the cockpit and peered through the windshield.

Two blue parachutes, disappearing into the clouds.

She laughed, a short, surprised bark.

Then she laughed again at the automated message that scrolled across the console: *Stay airborne. No calls. Back soon.*

"What is it?" CaLarca had followed her. "Is that- what are they doing?"

"Leaving," Sydel said. "I suppose it was inevitable."

"They just left? Without telling us?"

"Seems that they did."

"And I'm just to continue flying around in circles?"

"I guess so."

"Do you not find it slightly frustrating," CaLarca said, sitting down hard in her seat and smacking her fist on the console, "that she keeps leaving us behind to fend for ourselves?"

"She's not thinking of us," Sydel said. "She's thinking of him."

CaLarca said nothing, but she gripped the controls with enough force to strangle a person.

Sydel stared at the clouds. Phaira and Theron. Unexpected. But at the same time, not. How curious.

"What are you smiling about?"

Should she say what she knew? Sydel had a strange urge to share in her glee, to gossip just a little about something other than death. "Phaira and Theron."

"What about them?"

"When you clear away all the complications, they do seem to be an uncanny fit."

CaLarca made a face. "Those two? Don't be ridiculous."

"Why is it ridiculous?"

"Well, they're both criminals, to start," CaLarca sneered. "And self-absorbed, and full of excuses, so I suppose, yes, they might be perfectly happy together, killing anyone who doesn't agree with them. If it's anything between them, it's lust and boredom, nothing else."

Sydel glared down at CaLarca. "And you are so certain, of course."

"I'm far older than you. And married for nearly your life-time. I know of what I speak."

But Sydel's temper had been shaken loose. "So there's only one true kind of love, then? Your arranged, very convenient, very dull marriage with Ganasan?"

CaLarca started, as if shot. "Don't you dare to -"

"I can, and I will," Sydel interrupted. "Phaira is my friend. Don't speak ill of her."

"At one time," CaLarca reminded her. "We were friends, too. I told you things I never told anyone else, I let you see into my mind and my memories."

"You used your confessions to manipulate me," Sydel retorted.

"I did," CaLarca admitted. "I've grown to regret those choices."

"How useful for you, given that you have no place to go."

The sharp words were like knives, flung from her hip. Sydel felt a twinge of regret, at the pain she saw in CaLarca's eyes.

Then CaLarca lifted her chin. "We have an agreement, my husband and me. If there were ever danger, from the NINE or any other threat, we would separate and go into hiding, and make contact when it's safe. I'm waiting for his signal. It's as simple as that. And if I have a place to stay in the meantime, then why not?"

"What's going on?" came Cohen's panicked voice from the doorway. "What's that alarm?"

CaLarca glanced over her shoulder. "Your sister is sleeping with Theron Sava," she informed him.

Cohen's chin jerked back. He looked to Sydel for confirmation. Taken aback, she felt her face flush, and she could only lift one shoulder in response.

Cohen blinked, and blinked, and finally turned on his heel and exited.

"You are a terrible person," Sydel hissed at CaLarca, following him outside. "The sooner you leave, the better."

Cohen was waiting for Sydel in the corridor. "Did they really leave us behind?" he asked her, with equal parts frustration and sadness, his arms crossed tightly in front of his chest.

She put her hand on his bicep. "Yes."

He huffed. "Never good enough, are we?"

"That's not what's going on," Sydel soothed. "Trust me."

"Where are they going?"

"Back to Lea, I believe."

Cohen's eyes flashed. "Then so do we. They can't just abandon us whenever they want. We have stakes in this. Lives we're trying to return to. It's not just about him."

Lives to return to.

He was going back to Toomba, to the grandmother, and the militia. Of course he was, she knew that he was, but for some reason, the news still stunned Sydel.

There was another beep, from deep inside the cockpit. Another call. Reluctantly, Cohen and Sydel ducked their heads in to hear the connection made.

"Is CaLarca there?" Anandi again.

CaLarca sat up straight in the pilot's seat, her black eyes wide. "Yes," she finally spoke. "Just tell me. Ganasan was captured?" The words were slightly strangled.

"No."

Everyone turned to the speakers.

"I'm so sorry," Anandi was sputtering. "I'm so sorry to be the one to send you this, but..."

A translucent screen unzipped above the console, a grainy picture growing clearer.

Two bodies, burned beyond recognition.

The shape of a man, and a child.

A loud bang echoed through the cockpit, as CaLarca slid from her seat to the floor.

PART FOUR

When the call disconnected, it took a long time for Renzo to speak again, anger burning in his chest.

"Kuri," Renzo finally spat out. "What do you know?"

In the co-pilot seat of the *Arazura*, Jetsun's perfect face seemed to crumble, just a little. She quickly slid it back into place and tossed back her hair. "Not much."

"What - do - you - know?" Renzo snapped, emphasizing each word. There wasn't time for her stupid, haughty behavior. Bad enough that she'd called him, whining about the heat and asking for a pick-up, when the *Arazura* wasn't even fully repaired yet.

Jetsun lifted her chin, though her eyes remained down. "From what I understand," the woman finally said, "a trade was made in Toomba, when you and your family captured Kuri Nimat, and when he was sent into the mountains. Theron took custody of him."

"Why?"

Jetsun's golden eyes flickered to the left. "Information."

"Is he dead?"

"I believe so."

"Where is his body? Did you dump it in the river or something?"

"I don't dispose of bodies," Jetsun snapped. Then she sobered. "But I have an idea. You have to understand, when Iyo

Sava died, and Theron was announced as the successor, he disappeared."

"What do you mean, disappeared?"

"We couldn't find him for five days. Bianco was going crazy. We had people everywhere looking for him. One of his bodyguards finally tipped us off. Theron had drafted him for a specific project, which had just ended. Then Theron emerged, ready to take the helm."

"And what was he doing in those five days?"

"I've never quite had the courage to ask. But the bodyguard, Grey, he did tell me where they had been."

She gestured at the *Arazura* console. "Though we can't go in this. Too conspicious, plus it will sink in the mud. I can have a towncar here in thirty minutes."

"Why didn't you do that in the first place?"

Again, the woman's face faltered a little. "Maybe I didn't want to be alone."

Renzo cast her a sidelong look. Then he let it go. "Fine. Call whoever, and - "

"Come with me to the skerries?"

"Which ones?" Renzo asked, surprised. "In Lea? Why?" Lea was one of three coastal cities affected years ago, he remembered, when a meteor broke into three parts in the atmosphere, hit the ocean, and swallowed up miles of inland cityscape. The leftover, abandoned buildings, the sunken streets, five miles inland in each city were now walled off, and referred to as the skerries. He'd only seen the ones in Daro, his hometown, and then only from a distance.

"Just come with me.." There was a hint of plantiveness in that request.

Renzo stared at her. "You guys have secret bases there or something."

"Or something." Jetsun stared through the windshield of the *Arazura*. "So I've been told."

* * *

Cohen and Sydel managed to keep the *Mazarine* on autopilot, and entered in the coordinates for Lea, the center of the capital city. CaLarca was no help; she had been sitting in the corner of the cockpit for the past hour, her head in her hands.

"I had an idea." Cohen said under his breath to Sydel. "About the Red. You're not going to like it, though."

"Just say it." CaLarca's voice was a low, drunken mumble.

"Phaira shot that Red before, and it did no good. But in Kings Canyon, you guys could infuse weapons, right? With energy, so they were more powerful? Maybe it's the kick needed to make an impact." He glanced at Sydel again. "Have you ever fired a gun before?"

Sydel shuddered. "No, and I don't dare to."

"I could do it, I guess, if you get it ready for me."

"It won't be the same," Sydel interrupted. "Huma told me. Even if I infuse it, when I pass it to you, it immediately starts to lose its power."

"I will do it, then."

Sydel and Cohen turned to stare at CaLarca, who had risen to stand. Her braids were a mess, her white face was flush, but her black eyes were dead.

"You just channel Nadi into a firearm," CaLarca stated, her voice a monotone. "And then fire. That's it?"

"Yeah, but have you ever fired a gun before?" Cohen asked.

"No. What do you have on board?"

Cohen frowned. "My Vacarro, but I don't think a sniper rifle is going to work. You need something small, but powerful."

"Phaira has her guns somewhere, right?" Sydel suggested. "The Calises? I haven't seen them in a while, but..."

Cohen made a face. "You don't want to touch those things. The kickback is brutal, it'll dislocate your arm. The only reason she hangs onto them is because she's sentimental."

The three looked at each other, and all seemed to have the same thought at the same time. Theron must have something, somewhere, stored on this ship. But they would have to go digging into all corners. He wouldn't like that.

"I don't care," CaLarca's voice broke through Sydel's thoughts. "Let him hate us. I'll find something to use. Just teach me."

She was quiet for a few moments. "If I'm focused on infusing," she started again, "it means I can't split my efforts. Last time, I caught the energy around its body, and kept it in place until everyone could get into the escape pod. I can't do that if I'm doing this."

"Then I will," Sydel said. "Though I've only ever generated within. I haven't actively tried to control another person's Nadi before."

CaLarca's eyes glittered, in a way that made Sydel want to run. "Then I will teach you."

* * *

When Phaira and Theron landed on the city outskirts, abandoning their parachutes, they quickly set off for the nearest town. A few connections, and they were finally on the bullet train, zipping through the landscapes, on the way back to Lea. Private cabin, Phaira had insisted. And when Theron protested, she pointed out that she was paying for it, so his bank activity couldn't be traced. She did her best not to wince at the amount of rana she had to hand over.

Now she sat with a bottle in hand, sipping at the bittersweet cider. Cold lips, cool palms. Taking stock of her surroundings. As long as she kept her back to the wall and her eyes on the door, they should be safe as they worked out their plan. She wondered when this was all going to stop. How this was all going to end up. She wasn't particularly afraid of death, but it was more the burning curiosity to understand the threat in its entirety. She couldn't die without taking that thing with her.

"Don't you want a glass?" Theron was asking her. He was seated across from her, one long leg folded over the other, arm stretched along the back of the seat. Only his foot, bouncing just a little, gave away his anxiety.

She tipped the bottle in his direction. "Maybe you should have one."

Theron shook his head, watching the landscape outside. They had one hour before they hit Lea. It seemed like a thousand, stretching ahead. This was all I wanted, not so long ago, she reminded herself. But she felt weirdly shy, now that it was just the two of them. When there was no physical affection, what else was there?

Somehow, her mouth opened, and she began to ramble, to fill up the empty space. She told him about what she'd experienced over the past weeks. That interrogation room with Ozias and the shapeshifting Kuri; spending the night in Jetsun's apartment; Yann and the officers descending on Toomba, held back by the mountain militia, which Cohen had apparently joined. How CaLarca was still living with them, yes, but it was only a shaky alliance in order to root out the rest of the NINE; how Phaira hadn't trusted the green-haired woman from the start, and she still didn't.

He listened without commenting. His golden eyes flicked over to hers every once in a while, but then returned to stare out of the window.

Finally, she ran out of things to say. Only fifteen minutes had passed. Now what?

Cheeks burning, she slumped down in her seat and activated her Lissome and spread out the digital details of every death in front of her, scanning each picture, looking for something other than the obvious connection to Theron. Bodyguards. The guests at the party. Bianco.

"Tell me about Bianco."

"He was my grandfather's closest friend. Often the one paying attention to me and my cousins, when Iyo was busy. Tough, and frustrating, and stubborn." He paused then. "Why?"

"Did he support you?"

"How do you mean?"

"Was he on your side, so to speak?"

"Well, yeah. When my grandfather died, he became my advisor. His sole purpose was to make me a leader." Phaira caught the sarcasm in that statement. "Why?"

Phaira revolved the pixelated image to face Theron: a mass of blackened bone and ashes. "His death was different from the others. They were all left with lethal wounds, left to bleed out and be discovered."

"He was in pieces," Theron corrected.

"But his corpse was also burned in the alleyway," Phaira pointed out the charred remains. "Why the extra step?"

Theron was silent.

"That's our first stop in Lea," Phaira finished, sweeping all the projections back into the Lissome. "His place. I want to know all about him."

"Maybe he fought back, and it made the Red angry," Theron said. "He wasn't a pushover. And he was the most loyal man I've ever met. "

"Stop being sentimental; you didn't like him, anyways." Phaira retorted. "And what's loyalty mean in your family?"

That stung him. But he didn't deny her words.

She leaned forward, her wrists on her knees, her head tilted so she could look into his eyes. "Hitmen don't just strike without researching every minute detail. This Red knew your schedule, your set-up, where you live. How did they know any of it? Someone is talking, and maybe it was Bianco. I've thought so for a while now."

Theron didn't say anything.

"It breaks the rules, right?" she queried. "Tarnishing his memory?"

"It's not quite that dramatic," Theron said dryly. "But people were more loyal to him than they ever were to me."

"So we take advantage of your position," Phaira said. "And my talent for persuasion."

A slight smirk appeared on his face. "Quite the team."

"We'll see now, won't we?" Phaira grinned back. "Just try to keep up.

"You know," he said, his smile dropping. "I got in a lot of trouble when I got back from Liera. Gone for a week, almost killed the guards who came looking for me."

Uneasy, Phaira sat back. She remembered every detail of that week in Liera, the nights in his company, more than she would ever admit. And yes, she recalled how, again and again, he'd mentioned that his grandfather would be looking for him. And yet he stayed with her, night after night.

"Well, Bianco administered the punishment, under my grandfather's direction," Theron said. "He froze my accounts. Placed me under house arrest, like I was grounded. Had to do menial labor and make deliveries. Took some smacks upside the head. It was like they didn't know what to do with me, like they only understood how to punish a child. And I let him beat me. I did nothing, like I always do."

He glanced at her. Phaira realized she was wincing.

"Why are you telling me this?" she asked, dropping her face into a neutral glaze.

"In the back of my mind, I've always wondered what it would take to make me let go of my control."

He turned to look out the train window again, a cold edge to his words. "I guess now I know."

* * *

The ride to the Lea skerries was quiet. Running his hands down the leather seats, Renzo wondered what Jetsun was thinking, as she gazed out of the window, her blonde hair like a wave down her shoulder.

"So why aren't you the head of the Savas? Why Theron?"

Jetsun cast a look at the driver, through the privacy glass. There was no sign that he overheard. "Why are you asking?" she said warily.

"Because you seem to be the one running the show," Renzo said. "And I'm curious why it's not official."

"Not qualified," she said loftily.

"Why not? Shouldn't it be the best person for the job?"

"And what makes you think Theron is the wrong person?"

"Didn't say that."

"Hmm," was her only response. "The answer is: I'm adopted."

"So? Does that matter?"

"It does to the Savas. They have strict ideas on their lineage. I serve a purpose, but I can only go so far." Renzo wondered if he heard bitterness in the blonde woman's voice.

"So who succeeds Theron? He doesn't have any other family, right?"

"He's the last legitimate heir. So the syndicate would implode, and there would be a scramble for leadership."

"You should know," she added. "We're being watched. By more than one set of eyes."

"By who?" Renzo yelped.

Jetsun crinkled her nose. "Law patrol. Detective Ozias, probably," she listed. "Some hired spies from some end of the Savas, tracking our movements."

Renzo looked around frantically. "We need to make another plan, come back at night -"

Jetsun shook her head. "I've been watched for most of my life. You just don't give them anything to use against you."

"Like the place where we are going?" Renzo hissed. "They'll arrest us as soon as we try to access the skerries."

Jetsun gave him a withering look. "They won't. And in this situation, it's to our advantage to be watched over."

They arrived at the barrier that separated the Lea skerries from the city. The wall was cement, and ten feet high, but there were hidden entry points, if one knew where to look, and Jetsun did. She pushed lightly on the cement, and a heavy door swung open. Renzo looked right and left, and in the sky, searching for signs of being watched. There were none.

On the other side of the barrier, Renzo squinted in the sun, taking in the view of several abandoned, crumbling apartment buildings, and signs marking each one as condemned. The ocean wind whistled through broken windows, a strange, eerie sound. Gravel crunched under their feet, along with the ashes of cigars and little fires, strips of cardboard with black edges, the popped-out eye of a doll or some other toy, rolling in a lazy arc in a puddle.

Jetsun stepped through the mess with ease, walking on the balls of her feet, her high heels hovering just above the mud, heading for a crooked house in the distance. She walked along the edge of the rotting stairs, and waited for Renzo on the porch. He peered over his glasses at the front door, bolted with rusty locks.

"He brought Kuri here?"

"So the rumor goes." She was waiting for something, running the edge of her thumb along her fingernails, back and forth.

"What's the problem?" Renzo said impatiently. "Get us in there, or get us out of here."

Jetsun bit her crimson lips. Then she let out a huge exhalation, and shoved her shoulder into it. The locks weren't sealed, Renzo realized, just lightly affixed for the appearance of security. The door swung into darkness: mold-covered walls, a staircase to the basement.

The smells changed as they descended, from rotten to clinical: bleach, and antiseptic, and a strange, metallic aroma that seemed to stick to Renzo's tongue. He felt along the damp, peeling wallpaper, straining his eyes to see.

The staircase opened into a basement, windowless, but lit in the corners. There were metal shackles attached to one wall, hanging limp, amid dried brown smears. Discarded wires with electrodes were strewn across the floor. A standalone console with a seat, several screens, measurement tools, discarded pens. A tiny closet, its door ajar. Horrified, Renzo peered inside. The walls were covered with fiberglass, with strange horizontal and vertical patterns. It smelled of sewage in here, and old sweat.

Someone had been shut up in there. He was growing more nauseous by the second, with every flash insight into what Theron had been doing in those five days. And by the look on Jetsun's face, she was experiencing the same level of distress.

"I didn't think he had it in him," Renzo said.

"Nor I," Jetsun confirmed, her voice strained. Not for the first time, Renzo wondered what the blonde woman really thought of her cousin.

A series of looming metal cabinets stood on the far side of the room. Four-by-four compartments. Handles freezing cold to the touch.

Renzo jerked one open and slid it back. Empty.

The next three, the same.

The fourth, he jumped back at the shock of white hair that appeared, as the light hit the inside of the drawer.

Kuri Nimat, at least a much older version of the man Renzo remembered. His lower body wrapped in a sheet. Scratches across the surface of his chest, his arms, his skin. Purple smudges under his eyes, skin sunken into his skull. Renzo peered underneath his head. The scalp was sagging, hastily stitched back together, more for neatness than any kind of healing. He could even see the faint white of bone through the severing.

"What is he thinking?" Jetsun was gasping, her hands to her chest. "Why wouldn't he get rid of the evidence? What am I supposed to do, now that I've seen, I can't - ?"

"That's your question?" Renzo snapped. "Not: why is there a dead guy being kept cold in some torture chamber, with his head sawed open?"

"Is he dead?" she flustered, looking crestfallen. "I thought we had a lead."

Renzo studied the body of Kuri Nimat. There was no breath, no pulse in its neck, and the skin had a sunken-in, waxy look. "He's dead."

"So we are back to nothing, then," Jetsun moaned. "No clues. No leads."

"Well, he had Kuri in here for five days," Renzo muttered, trying to remain clinical about it all, listing the facts. "Then Theron, or someone else, performed surgery on the back of Kuri's skull, for some reason. He was looking for something."

His thoughts turned. "He created the HALO with me. He sent me the proposal to start the manufacturing company for NINE-defensive equipment. His focus has always been on how to contain people with these abilities. Maybe he was trying to understand how Kuri's brain worked."

He glanced at Jetsun. "Maybe he's not finished with his research."

"But it's been weeks," the woman said weakly. "All this time, and -"

A BANG! from upstairs.

The two froze. "Who did you call?" Renzo hissed.

"No one," Jetsun snapped back.

Footsteps creaked over their heads. Whoever it was, they weren't trying to be quiet. The pace was casual, drawing closer to the stairwell.

Panicked, Renzo looked in all directions. There was no exit, other than the stairs that led them there.

A set of red boots appeared at the stop of the stairwell. A shadow stretched across the basement.

Before Renzo could blink, Jetsun had a gold pistol in front of her, trembling in her grasp.

Then the red silhouette appeared, shrugging with every step, a weird, jerking gesture, like an alien mimicking human traits. There was something large and round in its right hand.

"Stay back!" Jetsun ordered shrilly. "Surveillance is everywhere. You're trapped."

As if tossing a flower through the air, the Red sent its arm forward, letting the ball go.

It landed with a heavy wet thud in front of Renzo: dark, brown and black and red, spinning on the floor. Purple veins, white bone, ragged skin.

And a man's terrified eyes, staring up at Renzo.

* * *

"Squeeze the trigger slowly," Cohen instructed. "It's going to be loud, but you have to keep breathing."

CaLarca's black eyes narrowed at the target. Her arm muscles were more pronounced, Sydel noticed.

A shot fired, making Sydel jump. There was a hole in the paper target, thirty feet away, up in the left corner. At least she hit the paper.

"Better," Cohen said. "But here's the real challenge. Can you generate Nadi and still fire with accuracy?"

CaLarca closed her eyes, her finger grazing the edge of the Compact firearm unearthed in Theron's cabin.

Standing out of the way, Sydel kept her arms crossed tightly in front of her. *This is wrong, this is so wrong;* she couldn't shake the old, rigid thinking. The rules of Jala Communia ran deep, even with Yann gone. Even though her own morals were no better than lies, she still felt reverence for the gifts she had been given.

As Sydel watched, threads of green-streaked hair lifted from the woman's multiple braids, as if charged with static electricity.

The Compact fired. The paper target burst into flame.

"Whoa," Cohen gasped. "That really works?"

CaLarca was panting, her white skin even paler. "That takes a lot of Nadi," she remarked. "More than I would have thought. I don't know how many shots I can get off. Maybe three?"

"Better than nothing," Cohen said. "Slow the Red down, and Phaira and I take care of the rest."

"And me, too," Sydel heard herself say.

Both CaLarca and Cohen glanced at her. Then infuriatingly, at each other. Sydel felt her frustration bubbling up again. "Give me that," she ordered, gesturing for the firearm.

"Syd, you don't -"

"I do, and I will," she interrupted Cohen, snatching the pistol from CaLarca's hands.

"Careful!" Cohen yelped, his hands springing up. "Syd, don't just grab it like that, you have to check the safety."

Sydel gritted her teeth, and held the firearm in both hands. It was heavy, and still warm from CaLarca's grip. She braced her legs, rocking back and forth on her feet. Then she aimed at the target, which had cooled and stopped burning, and was now blackened with ragged edges.

Cohen shook his head. "That just looks wrong," he protested. "This isn't you, Syd, you know it's not."

"You are not helping!" Sydel snapped.

"You don't need his help," came CaLarca's quiet voice.

Yes, CaLarca had shown her that, in those weeks in Toomba. All the hours training, holding a plank position to improve her abdominal strength, to increase her physical strength and focus, all happening in the midst of her maddening, disintegrating mind. CaLarca had pulled her from darkness when she couldn't stop rocking in a tight ball, couldn't stop the thoughts layering in her head, telling her that she was worthless, soulless, murderous. CaLarca had cared for her like a mother.

She closed her eyes, and remembered the words spoken in training: *Tighten your muscles. Control the Nadi as it generates in your core. Strength is key to channeling it, to mastering it.*

A cool hand lay on her wrist, pressing down.

Startled, Sydel opened her eyes to see CaLarca.

There were faint lines on either side of the woman's black eyes, finely etched lines that weren't there before.

"Don't," CaLarca said. "Let me."

"I can do it," Sydel protested, shaking off her hand.

"I know you can," CaLarca said. "And better than me, I don't doubt it. But it will be far different when you're aiming that Compact at a living being, no matter how evil. If you hesitate, it'll be over. Your instinct is to use your gifts for good, not to channel them through another machine."

"And you won't hesitate?"

"No," CaLarca said. "I have nothing to fear."

* * *

The world shifted from black to a hazy yellow. His head was on the ground. His wrists itched; when he tried to separate them, the cold metal pierced his skin.

The sound of chains rippling. Renzo tried to see through his crooked glasses. He was on the floor, in that secret underground space of Theron's. He tasted blood in his mouth. His temples were throbbing. He smelled sweat, and harsh chemicals. He held back his coughing and sat up.

Jetsun was crumpled on the ground next to him, her hair ground into the dirt, so tangled and matted and smeared. She was bound at the wrists too, both of their chains attached to a bolt in the floor, like some kind of medieval torture dungeon. Was this really Theron's design? Was he behind this all along? How else would that thing, that Red, know where it was? What was it doing here?

With a shudder, he recalled the severed head of the man; one of the people charged with surveillance, no doubt. How many bodies were lying dead outside these walls, rotting in the sun? Someone would notice that the patrol wasn't checking in, that the Savas were missing in action.

Someone could come looking, find Renzo and Jetsun and rescue them. Phaira would. Theron would. They just had to hold on and stay alive until the raid.

He caught sight of the Red by the metal cabinets. Kuri's corpse was still rolled out, and the Red stood over him, staring down into his face.

Slowly, the Red removed the metal mask it wore, and unwound the cloth around its head. Shaved head, mottled skin, and underneath the metal mask, sharp jawline, angular nose. Feminine lips.

Female?

As if reading his thoughts, the Red turned to Renzo. They stared at each other for several seconds, the Red unblinking. Renzo couldn't summon the courage to even speak, or barely breathe. Woman or not, she was ripped with muscles; artificial, by all the stretch marks and discoloration. Veins protruded in her neck, by her temple. Bizarre, freakish creation. Man-made.

The blood hearts, he remembered. Drawn next to the bodies of the victims.

Heartbroken. For Theron?

"What did he do to you?" he burst out.

It was an enormous risk. But maybe if he just tried to talk, an idea would spark; maybe something would come to him; maybe if someone would blast their way through, to rescue them.

The words spilled out of him. "This isn't the way. I mean - I can see, clearly, that you're very upset, and you probably have good reason to be, I don't know, but - "

Was he really giving relationship advice to a mutated assassin?

"He's not worth it," he kept going. "You can still start over - "

The crack across his head made him blind for several seconds. White pain shot down his neck and spine.

"Renzo." A frightened voice behind him.

Through the blaze of his pain, he saw that Jetsun was awake, frantically pulling at the chains.

A shadow came over him. Renzo froze with fear. But it was Jetsun who cried out.

He twisted at the waist, yanking at the chains, catching sight of Jetsun's terrified gold eyes, before she was pushed into the padded room, the door slammed shut. Then the Red stared through the tiny window, as if fascinated at the sight of Jetsun's fists banging on glass with no sound.

He couldn't stop his teeth from chattering.

Hold on, he thought, wishing for the first time in his life that he were an Eko, that he could pass on his thoughts to Jetsun in that tiny, windowless space. *Hold on.*

* * *

Officially, there was no record of Bianco Sava as a child. He would have had a different surname back then, before he legally became a Sava and dyed his eyes gold. But there was no trace of his previous identity. The grandfather, Iyo, claimed they were friends from long ago, but by Phaira and Theron's research, there was no history of them attending school together, or weddings, or any kind of event. They even went to Lea's storage facilities, rummaging through his registered belongings. There was only remnants of Bianco Sava from the past twenty-odd years, in letters, cards, and photographs.

"How can there be no history on this guy?" Phaira asked, as they sat back, dusty, exhausted, and utterly confused. "You never looked?"

"I never saw the need to," Theron admitted, wiping dust from his brow. "He was just there, and always loyal. I never had any reason to suspect him of anything. No one did."

The last stop: Bianco Sava lived in an apartment in East Lea, one that Theron had never entered, because Bianco was always in everyone else's houses, offices, and condominiums. Theron checked a few times for the address, to make sure it was correct. But it was now in front of them: a five-floor squat box, wedged between two other complexes, with rusted ledges, peeling paint.

Staring at its angles, Phaira remembered what Theron had told her about Bianco. He had no children, no wife. He came to work for the Savas shortly after Theron and his cousins came to live with their grandfather. The grandfather, Iyo, brought him through the ranks, until Bianco served as his personal advisor. There were rumors that the two of them were gay, but nothing that anyone would admit to. Bianco was the mouthpiece for Iyo in trade affairs, black market arrangements, partnerships and terminations. Everyone knew him, everyone respected him, and secretly, it seemed that everyone thought that he would be named the successor to the Savas, despite his lack of blood connection. As Iyo's health began to deteriorate, Bianco travelled constantly on behalf of Iyo over the last ten years...

"There's a night guard," Theron's voice broke through her thoughts. "Might be more."

Phaira squinted. Theron was right. A man at the elevator, Phaira noted, giving a resident a quick once-over before allowing them to come in. "How do you want to handle this?"

"You already know what you want to do."

"Yeah, I do," she admitted. She craned her neck to look around the building, searching for the darker parts, the alleyway and the makeshift clotheslines. "5A, right?"

"Meet you there."

When Phaira reached the narrow alleyway, she vaulted from wall to wall, fingers gripping the stony edges, adrenaline rushing, springing back and forth until the walls began to narrow. Then she shimmed up, hands and feet alternating, using her upper body strength to propel herself up. It was a thrill to be set free from the confines of the ship, the hospital, to be out in the open, letting her body command her path. She counted up and across to the corner unit, and swung up onto the narrow balcony. The door was locked. Easily jimmied and slid open. She did so silently, tensed for any signs of someone within. There was nothing.

Inside, the space was silent, and dark. She activated her Lissome to project light, and swept it from side to side, picking her way towards the dark rectangle of the front door, watching for tripwires, alarms, anything that might set off a trap.

The sound of creaking, outside the door. Someone shifting in their position. Another guard. Why?

More and more, she felt certain that Bianco had something to do with all of this. Was he jealous? Phaira wondered. Surprised? Could he have betrayed Theron and set him up to be destroyed? If so, what went wrong? Why did the Red kill him and burn his body?

She heard the distant ding of the elevator. Phaira peered through the spyhole. Theron was outside the door, she could only see half of him, the other half of the circle taken up by the back of the guard's head.

"You know who I am," she heard Theron's low voice.

"Sir," the bodyguard replied. There was sarcasm in that voice.

Theron moved so fast that Phaira barely had the time to register the hold, as the bodyguard was wrenched to the floor, arm twisted behind him, wrist torqued to the breaking point.

Joint lock submission.

She'd taught Theron that.

And he knew it, from the way his eyes flicked to the spyhole, where he knew she waited as if he could see her mouth dropping open with surprise on the other side.

"Why are you here?" she heard Theron demand. "What's inside?"

"What? I can't - "

His words cut to a new gasp of pain.

"How long have you been stationed here?"

"Since Mr. Sava died."

"Why?"

"He ordered me to."

"When?"

"Before he died - he said that if someone came snooping after his death -"

There was a thunk, and the sounds of groaning.

"You listen to me," Theron instructed. "Say nothing to no one. If you do, I'll come back and take the arm off."

The door opened, and Theron's silhouette stretched across the apartment. His breath was quicker too; she could smell his perspiration. In the shadows, Phaira stared at him. How many people were out to betray Theron? No wonder he was such a mess.

They searched the apartment in silence. There were reams of paper, notebooks, scribbling in a language that Phaira couldn't read. Diagrams of the body, drawn in light pencil; notations of times and places, again and again. Bianco had been watching someone's movements. They continued the search, shaking open drawers, knocking on walls, flipping through books. There wasn't much.

Theron was looking underneath the mattress when he made a sudden grunt of discomfort, pulling out something from under his leg, and holding it between thumb and forefinger. Phaira squinted at the item.

Blue, round, smooth. A jewel.

No, a bead.

Phaira's mouth dropped open.

"What is it?"

Phaira snatched the bead from his hands, cradling it in her palm, flashing the light from her Lissome into it. She caught the faintest motion in the center of the bead: a swirl.

The same kind of bead from CaLarca's farm, found in the ashes.

She closed her hand around the bead, feeling it press into her bones. It made her shiver, just like the last time. Was Bianco the one who burned CaLarca's farm to the ground? Out of revenge? Out of some demonstration of loyalty to Theron? Was that one of his many business trips, seeking out the green-haired woman and destroying her life?

"Phaira."

She opened her eyes and looked down at the bead again. It had grown so heavy that it felt like it would push through her palm and emerge on the other side. Disturbed, she placed it on the floor. It spun a few times before settling, like there was life to it. "I've seen one of these before," she confessed.

"Where?"

"CaLarca's farm was burned to the ground weeks ago. One of these was in the ashes. I thought it was hers. I think Bianco might have been behind the arson."

Theron's hand closed around her wrist. Startled, she looked into the shadows of his face. He was looking in at the bead with horror.

Then she heard it: the hissing sound.

And she was sailing through the open door, into the dull yellow light of the hallway, past the surprised, swollen eyes of the guard, Theron's arms were around her as they hit the floor, skidding across the carpet.

But no explosion.

Untangling herself from Theron's grip, Phaira crawled forward, flinching in anticipation as she peered into the interior of the apartment.

Bianco's world was burning. A slow crawl of embers was spreading from the bead on the floor, sweeping over the sheets, the papers, the floors in a radial pattern. The bright orange line never burst into flame, but moved like lava, consuming everything. It was the creepiest thing that Phaira had ever seen. Was this what happened to CaLarca's farm? What was in that bead?

The sound of pounding footsteps; the bodyguard was headed for the elevator. Phaira was too dazed to stop him, and so was Theron, by the look on his face as he stared at the disintegrating apartment.

There were two beeps from both of their belts: Lissome calls. Theron turned away from her to answer. Phaira clicked the connection. "Who's there?" she called.

"It's Ozias."

Theron shot her a dark look. She lifted her eyebrows, daring him to say something.

"You should get to the Lea skerries now, and bring your team." Ozias's voice was gruff over the line. "Your brother Renzo and Jetsun Sava entered a building in there an hour ago, and my guy on surveillance isn't responding. Something is wrong."

Phaira's heart felt like it was being strangled.

"There's not much time before I call this in," Ozias continued. She could almost picture the detective looking from side to side, checking for eavesdroppers, by the swish of her breath. "Move fast. I can't condone anything but a clean capture. Don't give me a reason to come after you."

"Why haven't you already - ?"

But the line was already disconnected.

Next to her, Theron clicked his Lissome shut, his jaw was a hard right angle. "Because they'll raid the place, and leave no one standing," he answered her question. "

"Who called you?

"The man I sent to watch Jetsun isn't responding. We need to go."

* * *

Renzo spent the next hour curled into a ball on the floor, willing Jetsun to stay strong, and cataloguing everything he could possibly notice, smell, and hear from the Red, who never moved from her guard at the padded door. There had to be some weakness. Something to exploit. Something to turn off.

Like the cloaking mechanism. That was a major advantage; it was so quick to activate, it had to be similar to the stealthsuit he owned. There was some trigger that sent the electrical current through the clothing and shock it into invisibility.

Or the artificial parts of her body; whatever was in her chest, helping it to breathe. The Red was dependent on those areas to continue to function. Take away the cloaking, take away the artificial respiratory system, and they were still left with a violent assassin, but perhaps one on more equal ground.

Phaira could handle it. If she could find them. If they even realized that they were missing, and chained, and Jetsun was being tortured.

Suddenly, the Red moved. Terrified, Renzo watched as the Red jerked open the door she watched. Jetsun's body came tumbling over the threshold. There were tufts of blonde hair on the floor inside; she'd pulled out chunks. The smell of urine choked him. There were claw marks on her arms, and her breath came in shudders, one hand lifting to press into her forehead hard, shaking.

An hour did that to her? What was in there?

They were helpless. Utterly helpless.

Focus, he told himself. This Red was a NINE. He had been studying ways to break through NINE attacks for weeks. It was all in the brain, just waiting to be interrupted.

Hauling Jetsun up by the arm, the Red shoved her into a chair. The blonde woman moaned, her face covered with her tangled hair, as a strap was affixed across her chest, then her thighs and feet. Renzo yanked on the chains, again and again, the metal biting into the bones of his wrists. "Let her rest," he begged. "Let her sleep."

Overhead, floodlights flicked on, harsh and fluorescent, burning Renzo's eyes. Speakers crackled with static. Some kind of audio track was playing.

Then Renzo recognized the voices. Theron's low, growling voice. And Kuri, begging and pleading.

"Why bribe Sydel with money?"

"To pay to extract the implants... I was desperate... for Shantou and me, to be free of the pain..."

"We didn't know it was metal inside our heads. We broke into a facility with an MRI machine. Bribed a technician to take pictures of our skulls. The pin dislodged from her skull and ripped through her brain... I couldn't shut down the machine fast enough... And then we were reported, and barred. They from any hospital or facility. There were only underground surgeons, and hundreds of thousands of rana to have the procedure done..."

"Did Shantou survive?"

"She did." Here, Kuri let out a sob. "Please, let me go and take care of her..."

"Where is Shantou now?"

"I can't…. I won't tell you…"

"Do you know how many people you two have hurt?" Theron's voice was quiet, but furious. "It's not difficult to find your trail, when you know what you're looking for. So many people left with broken memories, reduced motor skill function, incapacitated. Typically blamed on a stroke or aneurysm, lucky for you…"

"Do you know what a Nyx is?"

There was a long silence. Then Theron spoke. "The second N in the NINE acronym."

"Nyx is control over another's actions, thoughts, words. They turn you into a husk, move you like a puppet. He got a hold of Shantou, and she let him experiment, do whatever he wanted, and I swore I'd get the money and get…"

As the voices reverberated through the basement, the Red wandered over to Kuri's corpse again. One clawed hand trailed the metal slab on which he lay.

Shantou. The Red was Shantou.

It wasn't a former girlfriend of Theron, exacting this revenge; it was Kuri's partner.

"Please," Jetsun rasped. "It wasn't me, I knew nothing!"

The Red let out a cry of pain, so harsh it made Renzo recoil. There was a clicking sound in the depths of her breath.

Then words came smoothly, without interruption, though muffled by the metal mask. "Why have you kept him in his position?"

Jetsun blanched. "I - what?

"Theron Sava is a disgrace to his position," the Red said. The sudden eloquence was almost as frightening as the silence.

"Embarrasses you. Causes you endless work. You know he's a poor choice for leadership. Yet you continue to enable him. Why?"

"I'm a Sava."

"Not a true Sava."

Jetsun let out a short, unexpected laugh. "Do you know to whom you're speaking?" she asked, some of that familiar haughtiness in her voice. "If you're looking to make me burst into tears, you're mistaken."

"Oh, we've already been down that route, haven't we?" the Red reminded her, with a meaningful glance at the padded room. "A proposition, then."

"What might that be?"

"Your release. Renounce your position, your faith, your family, and you can leave."

The Red couldn't be serious. This was a trick.

"Never," Jetsun snarled. "You're recording this conversation. If I make those statements, you'll make sure the world hears it, and it won't matter if I'm alive."

A bark of laughter behind the mask. "Another offer, then. Since you're such a dedicated Sava."

Renzo didn't like the tone in the Red's voice, how coy and teasing it sounded.

Nyx, he remembered from the recordings. *A husk to control. This isn't her voice. This is someone else's.*

"Kill Renzo."

His insides froze.

"Shoot him, stab him, whatever you want," the Red said smoothly. "Then you get to disappear."

She would do it. Renzo was certain of it, as soon as the words left the Red's mouth. Jetsun would do it to save her life. He didn't matter to her. This was the end.

The silence went on and on. Renzo refused to look at the blonde woman; instead he stared at the chains around his wrist, waiting for a click, for an explosion, for the unsheathing of a knife.

So it goes, he thought. *I didn't think this would be the end. I had so many plans, for when this was done.*

"I don't kill on your orders," Jetsun spat the final word, "Shantou."

Renzo stared at her. There was real fear in Jetsun's voice, and regret, but also gritted-teeth determination. She refused to look at Renzo, but she didn't need to. She had chosen Renzo's life. She'd spoken the NINE's name. Humanized her. Maybe that was the key, make her remember that she wasn't a monster, but someone who loved Kuri....

Then the world turned red.

* * *

"I warned you not to get involved." The woman's voice was full of ice. "And here you are again, calling."

"Anandi," Sydel said firmly into the black Lissome. "Renzo is in trouble -"

"And I warned him equally," Anandi interrupted. "Yet here you are, on Theron's goddamn ship, in the middle of a fight that I want no part of."

Sydel huffed with frustration. They were flying the *Marazine* as fast as they could to Lea, counting down the minutes until the arrival time. CaLarca and Cohen were in the cockpit, and Sydel had snuck away, hoping for one last resource of help.

"How many times does this have to happen, Sydel?" Anandi challenged. "You call me up in a crisis, expect me to work magic from a distance and save everyone? Is that my only purpose to the rest of you? Does it matter what I think or want?"

It was indeed her purpose, and it didn't matter what the girl wanted, but Sydel wasn't going to admit that outloud.

"You're better than this," the woman's voice jolted her back to attention. "You're better than what you're about to become, Sydel."

"You know, Anandi," Sydel said. "I'm very tired of people telling me what I should and shouldn't be. If you didn't care, you wouldn't be constantly watching everything that Theron does. And don't deny it, I know you are. Your father told me. In all those hours we spent together, helping him to regain his strength, while you were playing at being a revolutionary."

There was a long silence. Sydel winced at her own biting words. But they were already out there.

"For my own sake, and the Hitodama." Anandi finally spat out.

Sydel could sense Anandi's heart, how it beat faster with rage. Sydel's own anger was rising.

You owe me, she railed against the girl in her brain. *You owe us.*

Or I could make you, the tiny, sinister thought followed. Like pulling on a puppet's strings, a flicker of her fingers, closing her eyes, opening her brain. *I could make you do what I wanted.*

Where was this voice from?

"Get your Lissome tab on its throat or chest." The girl's voice was curt, and strained.

Sydel blinked. "What?"

"Lissomes are hyper-sensitive to heat. If they get too hot, too fast, the battery will blow. Send a charge, or use one of your NINE abilities. If it can't breathe, it can't fight."

Then Anandi's voice returned, higher-pitched, and shivering. "You're just like the rest of them," she hissed, a sob at the end of the sentence.

The line disconnected. Sydel stared at the Lissome.

Did I make her tell me that?

* * *

Renzo's cheek was freezing cold. Pounding headache. Stiff jaw. When he lifted his arm, his joints screaming in pain, to run his hands over his own head, all he felt was hair and skin. Nothing warm, nothing wet. He couldn't hold back the flood of relief, or the tears in his eyes.

Jetsun was face down on one of the cabinet's metal planks, next to Kuri's body, her wrists gathered on the underside, her legs fastened by straps. Her hands hung limp. Clumps of long blonde strands were on the floor underneath her. Renzo lifted his head, just a little, to catch a glimpse of the back of her skull: shaved to the skin, shockingly pale. The Red stood next to her, with a tray of tools, her clawed fingers tickling each instrument, as if waking them to life. There was a key on that tray, Renzo realized; for the chains?

The Red took up a scalpel in its clawed hands. Her eyes drifted over to Kuri's corpse, the ragged stitching visible underneath his white hair. He'd been black-haired, young, and handsome in Toomba. She didn't seem to care, running the back of her hand over his cheek. All of this death and destruction, over some idiot. And Jetsun was next. When word of her death got out, Theron would be blamed from coast to coast, with no one to defend him. The last step in destroying his reputation.

Renzo had to get help. He had to make someone know that they were in there.

What if I'm an Eko? he thought suddenly. *What if I try? Maybe if you want it enough, if you push hard enough, anyone can be an Eko.*

The thought was preposterous, even in his desperation, but he fought to believe.

SYDEL CALARCA PHAIRA ANYONE PLEASE GET HERE HELP US HELP US

The Red was cutting. Jetsun was screaming. And no one was coming through the door.

Frantic, Renzo wrestled with his chains, trying to angle his body to reach his prosthetic leg, to pull up the trouser. Jetsun's shrieking made him dizzy. His back cracked, and his neck wrenched. The bones of his hand ground against the restraints so hard he felt the skin split. Pain shot up his arms, but he kept pulling, until he finally got the hem and yanked that his trouser leg ripped.

The Red had noticed, the Red was turning, but he was already unclicking his prosthesis and reaching inside, withdrawing the slender tube within and shaking out the contents: a tiny explosive, sealed against any accidental trigger, and a silver coin with a dark center. He'd been working on it since Toomba. One single electromagnetic pulse. Enough to knock out a NINE.

He pressed the coin.

The Red jerked as if stabbed. It clawed at its head. Then it crumpled to the ground with a crash.

Jetsun was sobbing, the back of her head bloody. Renzo pulled with all his might at the chains. "Jet!" he cried. "Key. The key's on the tray!"

Jetsun rolled herself to a seated position, untangling her bonds, slipping her feet from the belts that held them. She was a pale, broken ghost, blood coating her shoulders like a cape, her hands lifting and falling, lifting and falling, like she didn't dare to touch, to feel what had happened at the back of her skull.

There wasn't time. The Red could wake up at any point. He tossed the capsule at Jetsun. "Put this on her," he told her. "Then get the key, and we'll get out before it's triggered. Come on, Jet, we're so close, please, wake up and move!"

Jetsun stared at the Red's back, its splayed arms. She scooped up the bomb with one trembling hand. Then she took the key from the tray, and slid it across the concrete floor.

Renzo snatched it and unlocked the shackles. Quickly, he twisted his prosthetic back into his right limb, and swinging his leg around, he hoisted himself to his feet.

"Come on," he urged Jetsun, looking back at her, hand outstretched, as he began to stumble up the stairs.

Their fingertips brushed.

A flash of light on metal, and Jetsun jolted backwards with a cry. Jetsun's ankle was caught in claws. The Red was rising behind her. But Jetsun still held the capsule.

Like she had been training for this her whole life, she flipped it open.

No, he pleaded with his eyes, frozen halfway up the stairs.

Jetson gave one stiff nod.

Then she turned and threw her arms around the Red's neck.

The blast blew him up the remainder of the stairs, the smoke rolling over him, choking him.

Then light burst through, and two pairs of hands took hold of him, four sets of fingers pulling him into the street. The sun blinded him. He couldn't stop coughing. The silhouettes were speaking to him, one low voice, one higher-pitched, but he couldn't make out the words or the faces.

"Shantou," Renzo gasped between strangled breaths. "It's Shantou! Shantou." His vision cleared for a moment; his sister hovered over him, her blue hair framing her face. He fumbled to grab her arm, bringing her closer, then pushing her away. "Get out," he wheezed.

"Where's Jetsun?" he heard over the roaring of his ears; the deeper voice, the black hair. Renzo's eyes were flooding with water, or blood, he couldn't tell, but he couldn't see, and he couldn't breathe.

* * *

The skerries were burning. Smoke, and fire, and rusted destruction, mud mixed with ash and mold. Holding onto Cohen's hand, still wincing from the echo of the blast, Sydel squinted through the wreckage, searching.

Three silhouettes, moving in the distance; a flash of familiar blue hair. Her hands flew to her mouth. Yes, it was Renzo on the ground, covered in blood and soot, his hands limp against the ground; Theron and Phaira were dragging him backwards, away from the blast, as smoke billowed out the door of the abandoned house. Cohen had released her hand, and was already running towards them. She saw Theron rise, then Phaira caught him by the arm. His broad back was the only thing that Sydel could make out, her eyes tearing from smoke in the air.

"Syd!" It was Cohen, yelling back for her.

She lurched forward, every step a jolt to her senses, the world growing closer in shaky focus. When she was close enough, she dropped to her knees and took hold of Renzo. Her leg grazed the metal of his prosthesis, hot to the touch from the explosion. His ears were bleeding, his glasses were broken, but thankfully the shards hadn't gone into his face. Abrasions. Quickened, but steady heartbeat. Her ear pressed to his chest; nothing in the lungs that she could hear. Head injury was likely, though, and they had to keep him steady, just in case...

"Jet?!"

Sydel lifted her head at Theron's exclamation. Yes, there was the outline of a body in the house's doorway, lurching through the smoke.

Separately, there was a sickening shift in the air: the release of death, Sydel realized. Someone had just died.

A *bang!* echoed through the skerries.

The silhouette crumbled to its knees, one hand curled around the doorframe. Covering her head, Sydel twisted to look behind.

CaLarca stood, Compact in hand, smoke from the barrel, energy glowing around her like sunlight. When she lowered the firearm, Sydel saw how pale CaLarca's skin was, how the Nadi dissipated, replaced with sickly yellow.

The open grief on the woman's face as the shadow collapsed in a noisy heap.

"Shantou," Sydel heard her murmur. "I'm so sorry."

Dropping the Compact, CaLarca ran past the group, pounding up the broken stairs to the porch.

Then there was a flash of black, and CaLarca flew backwards, scraping along the ground.

And Theron was on the porch, attacking, a flurry so fast that Sydel couldn't make out the difference between him and the Red, whose breath was strangled and who was growling, or who the splashes of red belonged to, with the smoke still billowing out the open door.

Sydel darted to CaLarca's side. "Come on," Sydel commanded, grabbing the woman by the arm, and forcing her to scurry backwards. CaLarca's hands covered her throat, as if to hold it together, as she stumbled over her feet, finally sitting in the mud.

"Let me see," Sydel instructed, pulling away her hands. No severed throat, as she feared, just four bloody horizontal lines. Theron had yanked CaLarca away just in time, so the Red's mad swipe with her metal claws only cut the skin, instead of severing jugular vein or esophagus.

As CaLarca panted, her fingers bloody, her eyes unseeing, Sydel grew aware of the presence of eyes. There were people watching them in the skerries, watching this fight between Theron and the Red: Ozias, the patrol, the Sava representatives, maybe cameras or Lissomes, held up to record the mysterious Sava leader, doing battle.

No one was coming to help. They all wanted to see what would happen next.

"She put Nadi into the bullets," Cohen was hissing at Phaira, as if he couldn't believe what he was saying. "And that thing is still alive, and fighting? How?"

"No matter," Phaira cut him off. "Get ready. You too," she turned to bark at CaLarca, who was just starting to lower her hands from her neck. "Take either side and close in."

"The Lissome," Sydel announced. "Get it on the Red's chest, under its clothes. I can overheat it from a distance, and it will explode and damage its breathing mechanism."

"How do you know that?" Cohen asked, shocked.

"It doesn't matter," Sydel said. "I will do it from afar when you give the signal."

Phaira was staring at her, but her words were in Sydel's mind: *Are you sure?*

Sydel gave one nod.

Phaira pulled her Lissome from her pocket. *Wait for my signal. Be ready.*

Then she ran, through mud and ash, and disappeared into the smoke and ocean wind.

* * *

The Red's metal mask was askew. One shoulder was split open, the muscle exposed. Welts and burns on her head, blood dripping down its arms, blue and black and viscous. Clicks and hisses sounded from its body, from the bullet holes that had punctured through her armor. The Red had avoided the brunt of the explosion inside, it seemed.

Give me the knife in your boot.

Phaira froze. It wasn't Sydel, though; it was CaLarca's haughty, shaking voice in her head. She saw the woman's green braids in her peripheral vision, flanking her on the left.

If you can get her pinned down, I can remove those claws.

Phaira unsheathed and tossed it at the woman, who caught it by the hilt. Cohen's red beard showed through the smoke for a split second, he was headed in the opposite direction.

Ahead, Phaira could make out Theron and the Red's silhouettes in the smoke. The Red had gotten Theron's face, though, and shredded through the cloth of his shirt, so it hung loose. His hair was unbound, and wild around his face. He moved so fast, and so aggressively, that it was almost frightening. He broke through the paneling with his fists, hissed when the claws caught him, bore down with his height and weight and wrestled the Red against the wall, into the porch, then, with a roar flipping her into the rail. It splintered around her and she scrambled away, slapping at her arm, as if to wake it up, and rolled backwards, into the mud, streaked and heaving.

Phaira, Cohen and CaLarca surrounded the Red, stepping onto driftwood and fallen rocks to keep out of the mud. The Red shifted from foot to foot, undulating its shoulders, eying the group. It had nowhere to go but the wreckage of the Lea skerries, or the open sea. Cohen's hands were in fists, his stance wide. CaLarca bore the knife like she had a thousand times before. Behind her back, Phaira rolled the Lissome between her fingers. She dared to look for Theron, just for a moment, and he was there, to her right, his back hunched, his face hidden by his loose hair.

As the Red turned in place, Cohen was the first to attack, leaping on the Red's back; he bellowed with pain as the Red dragged her claws down his forearm in three quick successions, and flipped Cohen away. Cohen sprawled into the mud, though he rolled quickly, avoiding the Red's follow-up stab into the mud with its claws.

Phaira was next, but before the Red could strike, she side-stepped, and let the Red go off-balance, then neatly crippling her knee, drove a back elbow into the back of the Red's neck, then joined her hands and smashed her fists into the side of the Red's face, just enough to push the metal mask askew. The Red howled, clawing at her face.

Masks. So stupid, Phaira couldn't help but sneer as she slid backwards in the mud, tasting salt in her mouth.

CaLarca was there, swiping with the knife. Phaira felt sudden, blinding heat, and two of the Red's clawed fingers fell into the mud, severed at the knuckle.

Then everything became a blur again. CaLarca was punched across the face. Phaira was kicked in the chest, so hard that it felt like her back was collapsing, but Cohen appeared behind the Red, snatching the Red's forearms and yanking them, just for the split second that he could, as Phaira surged forward and shoved the Lissome down the neckline of the Red's tunic.

Now, Syd! she yelled in her mind.

A sudden rush of heat; then, a crackle, and a burst of white light.

Phaira caught some of the current, flung backwards, all the air leaving her lungs.

Through her blurred vision, she saw the Red clawing at its chest, its severed hand tucked under an arm, the other scrambling to grab something, anything, to fix the tubes, to restore the circuitry now shutting down.

But there was a shadow over her now, as Theron rose, fixed his hands around the Red's neck and head, and wrenched with all his strength.

The *crack!* echoed through the skerries.

Theron flung the body into the mud and stalked after it, as if daring it to rise again.

The Red twitched, its eyes rolling, its mechanism still trying to work.

Phaira wobbled to her feet, feeling the jolts in her veins. CaLarca and Cohen were still.

Theron knelt down and stared into the Red's face, his features like stone.

The seconds dragged on. The sucking sounds carried across the Lea skerries.

Soon, there was only the whistle of wind.

It was over.

* * *

"I want the body," Theron said.

"Not an option," Detective Ozias said. Fire and rescue crews were incoming, estimated time of arrival within minutes. Still, Ozias and Theron argued, and as Theron thundered against her, Ozias seemed rattled, the first time Phaira had seen such a thing.

Renzo was awake, and Sydel was focused on dressing his wounds. Phaira's gaze travelled down the length of Renzo's body, the broken prosthetic, the burned and bloody trousers, the soot streaks across his face.

"Are you sure we shouldn't take him to a medlab?" she asked Sydel.

"He's stable," Sydel said. "Our best option for both equipment and discretion is the *Arazura*. If my clinic is still stocked, I can heal him."

"Cohen will help you," Phaira instructed. "CaLarca can fly you to the *Arazura*. Get you guys out of sight." She kept glancing over at Theron, wondering what he was thinking. It looked like some kind of resolution had been found with Ozias. The two had stepped apart, Theron surveying the house as Ozias talked into her fist, her eyes darting around, checking for incoming traffic. CaLarca and Cohen were guarding the body. Cohen was dark and grim; CaLarca was pale and listless, looking like she was about to blow away. Like the dying smoke from inside the house; Jetsun inside, dead and smoldering.

Phaira started to make her way into the fire, intent on bringing the woman to the outside, in whatever condition she was in.

Phaira, Sydel's soft voice came into her head. *You can't do anything for her.*

Phaira stopped and scowled at the ground. What about respect? she wanted to argue. What about seeing Jetsun Sava as a person to be respected, rather than just collateral damage? Memories swirled through Phaira's brain, of staying on house arrest in Jetsun's townhouse, the little insights, the surprisingly fierce way that she cared for Theron. Another one dead for a terrible reason.

If you want to help, take him away. Sydel's voice drifted through her head again. *Give him the space he needs to grieve. He will fall, soon, I fear, and it may be terrible.*

Rattled, Phaira glanced at Sydel. "Who?" she mouthed, feigning ignorance.

But the girl gave her a knowing look.

Embarrassed, Phaira cleared her throat and turned to CaLarca and Cohen, as they drifted towards her.

"How is he?" Cohen asked Sydel.

"He'll be better in the *Arazura*," Sydel said out loud. "We should go."

Crouching down, Cohen lifted Renzo easily in his arms. His older brother stirred a little, a hand coming to his forehead. Phaira helped Sydel to her feet.

"Stay hidden, just in case of backlash," Phaira told the group. "I'll stay and get him home safely, and close out our contract. I'll call shortly."

Everyone turned to leave, save for CaLarca. Her eyes were black and hollow, red around the rims. Her shoulders were concave. There was no anger, or coldness or frustration anymore. She was empty.

But before Phaira could say a thing, CaLarca had turned away, to follow the rest of the group.

* * *

The *Mazarine* docked next to the *Arazura* in the tall parking garage, where Renzo had left the ship only hours earlier. Disembarking, Cohen carried Renzo in his arms, striding across the concrete without a look back. Sydel did the same. She was glad, somehow, to leave the *Marazine* behind.

Inside the *Arazura's* medical bay, Sydel did a thorough examination of Renzo's body, searching for any signs of internal damage. Renzo was hooked up to machines to measure his vital signals, treated for his burns, given intravenous fluids and pain medication. His broken glasses were on the table next to the bed; he looked younger without them, the lines on his face less pronounced. He would have hated it, but Sydel couldn't help but gently sweep his blond bangs off his forehead. A trace of soot remained on her fingers. She registered the urge to wipe it, and moved through the curtain that separated the space.

On the other side, in her cabin, Cohen had changed his clothes, and was now sitting on her small twin bed, looking through train schedules on his Lissome. Sydel's chest sank. It was only hours since the awful incident. Was he already planning to leave everything behind? She sat down beside him, her eyes on the floor.

"When are you leaving?" she asked quietly.

Cohen shook his head. "I'm not sure yet, but I'm not staying. And I don't think you should, either."

Deep inside, Sydel felt a flash of anger. *Everyone is always telling me what to do.*

"I'd ask you to come back with me," Cohen added, shyness creeping into his voice, "but I doubt you want to live in Toomba."

"Are you asking me?"

"Well, yeah," Cohen said, a tired grin creeping onto his face. "Of course. You're my girl. I always want you near."

A warm, pleasant wave coursed through Sydel, and she blushed, smiling at the floor.

But her smile soon faded. What would she do in Toomba? Another community in isolation, separate from the rest of the world. There was already a medical clinic on the mountain; would they give her a job? Would the grandmother accept her? What if she became as powerless and insecure as she was in Jala Communia, caught up in the same groups of people, prejudices walling her in?

She looked into Cohen's hesitant face, those familiar, boyish eyes underneath that red beard. More than with anyone else in the world, she felt safe, and understood, and cherished with him. It was the first time she ever felt like that. Maybe it would balance everything else out. Community, maybe, instead of a prison. A home to build. Maybe a family, someday. Maybe those were things that she wanted. A legacy. What name would she go by, enmeshed in the civilian world? She had no legal surname.

But she still had the right to a very powerful one.

Cohen's face was very near to hers. Reflexively, she ducked her chin. Then she chastised herself for the reaction.

Cohen, however, just smirked. "Why do you do that?" he asked her. "Is it the beard?"

"I don't want to be bad at kissing," she murmured, hotly embarrassed.

Cohen intertwined his big fingers in hers. "Not possible. But no guy ever came after you?"

"Yann kept a firm hand on my activities," Sydel said. "There wasn't much time for socialization." She looked down at her feet again, gathering her courage.

"Cohen," she began. "I'll come to Toomba."

Cohen's face broke out in a huge grin. He went to sweep her into his arms, but Sydel held up her hands. "But first, I want my name. I want to be legally recognized as the daughter of Joran Asanto and Tehmi Shovann."

The sparkle in Cohen's eyes dimmed. "Are you sure you want to do that? They'll fight you hard, from what everyone's saying."

"I want to belong somewhere. I want a history."

"You have a history with me."

"More than that, Cohen," she told him gently. "I want to know who my parents are, who they really were. And what they did in Kings Canyon and beyond. And to pry open those vaults, I think I need to stake my claim."

Cohen nodded. He looked a little disappointed, the fingers in hers more slack. She gripped them and brought them to her chest. "But I can't do this by myself."

Cohen squeezed her hand. "You're smarter than all of us, Syd. Of course you can do this."

"I feel confident that I can do it, if you are with me, Cohen."

Finally, that half-grin came back on his face. "Well, all right, then. Asanto Foundation, watch out."

* * *

It took Phaira almost an hour to convince Theron to leave the skerries, to leave behind the Red's corpse for Ozias to process and cover up, to leave Jetsun's body for the authorities to recover. He'd left specific instructions on where Jetsun was to be brought, what would be done with her, enforcing non-disclosure agreements with the arriving coroner and officers. They seemed to understand, and agree, strangely enough. This was a serious situation. The death of Jetsun Sava would be an incredible breaking story. People would be descending on Theron, demanding answers, demanding access to her accounts, and reassurance that all the secrets she collected over the years would go with her to the grave. Theron didn't need to tell Phaira this. She also knew what it was like to deal with the waves of attention after a death, the food, the discomfort, the screaming longing to just get away from all the sympathetic eyes, touches, greedy side glances.

The train slid to a gentle stop. Central Lea. Theron had been silent for the past hour, turned away from Phaira. There was still blood streaked on his clothes, and his hair was still loose and tangled. People were staring, but he didn't seem to care. She hesitated before taking his arm, leading him carefully to the exit and to the underground passages. He let her, surprisingly.

They took underground tunnels, sleek and silver and air controlled, making their way to the section of exclusive luxury apartment buildings where Theron lived. For once, the vacuous space was a comfort; being in members-only tunnels meant there were limited dangers to consider. If there were any at all. Who could say? Phaira was still reeling from the past few hours. The discoveries, smells and memories. The anger blazing on Theron's face, how vicious and fast and cold he was.

There was no one in his building, not in the lobby, the elevator, nor the hallways. The faintest outline of blood remained on the carpet, just outside his door.

Theron stood at the threshold, staring at the peephole. Phaira waited, watching his back. Finally, he keyed in his code and pushed through the door.

For a moment, Phaira wondered if he might slam the door in her face. She wouldn't blame him, not really, if he did. But the door was left open and she took the invitation.

The apartment was cold. The curtains were drawn, the lights were off, and Theron made no move to make any changes. His feet dragged as he made his way through the living room. Phaira closed the front door behind her. Then she leaned her back against the wall, her heart thrumming, watching as his silhouette disappeared through the half-open door of his bedroom. She heard the running of water and the sound of splashing, followed by the squeak of a mattress; he was on his bed.

Best to leave him to it. At the very least, she could sweep the apartment and make sure nothing had changed. In the wake of Bianco's mystery, and Jetsun's death, she was even more certain that there were listening devices or other mechanics keeping track of Theron's whereabouts. He didn't need to know about it, unless she found something.

Phaira ran her hands over the ragged edges of the tear in the wall, the ventilation gates, the furniture. There were locked drawers that she immediately wanted to look into. Maybe if he fell asleep, she reasoned. The key was around somewhere. Was he asleep?

She took off her boots and crept towards the open door, peering around the edge of the doorframe. He was flat on his back, face angled to the ceiling. Phaira couldn't tell if he was actually sleeping; his chest rose and fell, and his eyes were closed.

"Theron."

His eyes flickered. He didn't turn his head, though.

Phaira hesitated. Even with everything that had happened, she yearned to draw all that bitterness away with her body. Maybe it was all too much to ask. Maybe it was a fool's game, to still be thinking like this, for someone like him.

Still, she came into the bedroom and slowly lowered herself onto the edge of the bed, her feet piqued and ready to run. She touched the back of his hand, still damp from the water. He didn't move.

Gathering her nerve, she slid her fingers around his, feeling the scars on the inside of his palms, rough and familiar. She lifted his hand, heavy and warm. He still didn't react.

With a burst of courage, Phaira grazed her cheek against the back of his hand. It felt incredibly daring, coupled with her vulnerable thoughts as she shut her eyes. *I've missed you. I've missed you so much.*

"I'm sorry," she whispered instead.

His wrist turned against her mouth. Fingertips stroked her jawline, from ear to throat. Then his palm settled against the curve of her face.

When she opened her eyes, he was sitting up, his right fingers wound through the hair at the back of her head, the edges of his left fingers in her back, like hooks pulling her in. His lips were wet, but still they burned her, like a blaze across her mouth, knocking aside her control.

Cold fire bristled over the surface of her skin, every cell alight and hypersensitive from the pressure. Their quickened breath echoed through the space. His hands slid under her shirt. His breath was in her neck, her blood was being shot through with ice, and she was falling back, yanking at his shirt, relishing the shock of his hot skin, the edges of his hair on her ribs. The bitter relief of his body and fingers and mouth, violent and desperate, her thoughts were a jumble of ecstatic and frantic.

Is this what it was like, back in Liera when I came through the window, trying to forget all the pain in my head?

Did I burn him, too?

* * *

Light pierced through a crack in the curtain, rousing Theron from a dreamless sleep. He sniffed and winced. His whole body ached: scratch marks on both his arms and chest, the deep bruises, the left side of his face.

Then memories floated back, as if remembering a dream. Jetsun. The Red. Phaira.

Groggily, he swept his arm across the bed, searching for her cool skin.

There was nothing. He was alone.

He pressed the heel of his hands into his eyes. The old thoughts were automatic. *Of course she's gone. She was always going to leave. What, you thought she'd really stick around when this was done? She's not interested in your stupid -*

The sound of rustling in the other room.

Theron sat up on his elbows, wincing again as his joints protested. Then Phaira strode through the doorway, wearing one of his dress shirts, her hair a thousand shades of blue in the dusty sunlight. "How can you live here and not have glasses?" she asked him. "There's barely anything in your cupboards. What do you do, just use your hands?"

Relief coursed over him. Still, he feigned casualness. "You're not looking in the right places, obviously," he quipped back. "I have lots. Somewhere," he added, suddenly unsure. He never ate in the apartment. And she was right, he did use his hands most of the time.

She smirked at him. Then her smile faded. "Lots of calls coming in," she said, leaning against the doorframe, her hip cocked to the side. "I should probably get out of your way. Go check on Renzo."

Not yet. He didn't dare to say the words aloud, but there they were. *Not yet.*

He flung the covers off, ignoring the pain in every limb, got to his feet, and strode across the bedroom to a very surprised Phaira.

But when he came to stand in front of her, he froze. He didn't know what to say, or what to do, as the same thought hammered through his head: *Don't leave me alone. Don't leave me alone.*

Through the open collar of her shirt, he caught a glimpse of the pink flush at the base of her throat, the remnant of so much blood-rush the night before, beautiful, and lingering, caused entirely by him. He wanted to focus on that. He didn't want to think about Jetsun's body and burial; the mess of meetings he would have to undertake; the inevitable questions from Ozias and the rest of patrol, once they realized that they had him by the throat...

She was the first to move. The sudden weight of her body pressed against his, soft tendrils of her hair against his cheek, standing on the balls of her feet, her arms strong around his neck. An embrace, so tight that he could feel the movement of her ribs as she inhaled.

Lust was bubbling up in him again, but he pushed it down, and instead chose not to move or speak, and to just drink in the sensation of being held, for as long as it might last.

* * *

Soon, too soon, she reluctantly dressed in her old clothes, stained and bloodied as they were, and headed into debriefing with Ozias at the Lea patrol station. She promised Theron that she would keep things private, and asked him to meet her under the East-West Lea bridge when she was finished, so she could fill him in. She kissed him, gripping the front of his shirt. Then she smiled at him, a little shy, and gave an awkward hand wave as she went through the door.

When he heard the ding of the elevator door, Theron punched in the cc to the *Arazura*, neatly bypassing all the securities installed.

The connection was made, and a screen opened; Sydel's coppery skin on the other side, with an ashy tint to it, from fatigue and who knew what else.

"Is Renzo alright?" he asked gruffly.

Sydel's eyes, so close to the screen, peered at him like she knew all his thoughts. "Yes," she finally confirmed. "Are you?"

"I need to speak with him."

"Briefly. He needs his rest."

"Understood."

The Lissome swiveled to show Renzo's tired face, bandage over his forehead, gray-green eyes piercing through the screen. For a moment, Theron faltered. He hadn't considered Phaira's reaction in his decision, just what could be accomplished. She might be upset. But it was too late now; Renzo was eying Theron with impatience. "What's going on?"

"Can we speak privately?"

Renzo said something off-screen. A few seconds later, he lifted one blond eyebrow. "Well?"

It was painful to say the words. "What happened in there, with you and Jet? I need to know."

Renzo ran a slow hand over his face. "I don't even understand half of what I saw in that basement of yours."

"Yes, you do," Theron challenged. "Same goal as you. Trying to find a way to stop the NINE from hurting anyone else. So, what did you use to get away?"

Renzo paused for a long while. Then: "Electromagnetic pulse coin, one-shot deal to disrupt NINE brainwaves and make an escape. And a miniature explosive, kept in a safe cylinder to avoid triggers. Kept both in my prosthesis since Toomba."

"Your creations?"

"Obviously."

"Yet you never signed the papers to release the patents, and start manufacturing." With a pang, Theron recalled their meeting in Jetsun's office. It would have to be cleaned out, and quickly. "You have a change of heart?"

"No." Renzo's voice was hard. "I don't want to sign over my designs. I want to partner."

"You don't need to be involved on that level," Theron warned, holding back his surprise. "Just stay remote. "

"No," came Renzo's sharp retort. "I want to partner. People need protection against these NINE. What happened to me - it's not happening to anyone else."

I should say no. I should disconnect this call. I should insist that Renzo think about it.

But it was what he'd always wanted; a partner. Someone with the same goals, someone who thought the same and worked well with him.

Theron remembered the feel of the Red's neck in his hands, the crack and snap, the satisfaction in watching the life go out of her eyes. He was a Sava, after all. The realization was both horrible and a relief, in a strange sense. But he would be a better Sava, with greater intentions. And Renzo's declaration, his willingness, it meant he was on the right path, didn't it?

A thought crept in, like a crack of light. *Phaira will hate me.*

"Well?" Renzo prodded. "I need some time to recover, but as soon as I can, we should meet up and review strategies."

Theron weighed his memories of Phaira, both in the past, and minutes ago. The week on the house on the cliffs. The nights in Liera. The way she gazed at him when she left this morning. How, despite his anxieties, his insistence on staying remote, a heaviness lifted off his chest when she was nearby, and some form of peace was in its place, nipping at the edge of his hopelessness. He'd fallen for her from the start, if he were honest with himself, her aggressive, vulnerable, valiant self.

But what he felt, or what he thought he felt, it didn't matter. It was all a disaster in the making, he couldn't deny that.

You know she'll leave you behind eventually, his reason told him. *The dream always ends.*

Renzo's inventions are for the greater good. They're more important. Focus on that.

"I'll be here," Theron finally spoke. "I'm ready. Just say when."

* * *

Half of the bulbs on the East-West Lea bridge were burned out, the rumble of cars mixing with the rush of water. Grit and gum scraped under Phaira's feet. The silent core of the city a kilometer away down the riverside.

A crackle of a branch underfoot, from afar. Phaira's body flooded with impatience. Still, she didn't move from her stance, hands in pockets, watching the river. Only when the sound of his shoes that slid, instead of scraped, against the rough platform, when his light gait grew clear with every movement, and she felt his shadow over her, did she turn around with a smile.

It left her face, though, at his stoic expression. Theron's hair had been neatly tied back; all traces from the battle yesterday were gone from his face. He looked severe, and watchful, and unapproachable.

Cautious, she stepped away, until the cold metal railing dug into her tailbone.

"I didn't tell Oz anything," she finally spoke. "I never would, you know that."

"What did she ask?"

"What we have been doing over the past week. If it were true that you had been hospitalized - I said no."

If we were involved, she thought, but didn't say outloud.

"How we knew to find the Red in the skerries, and her true identity. That, I told her, since it's public knowledge now, the whole NINE thing. She's going to be calling us. But we can decide what we want to share."

Theron nodded.

Growing cold, Phaira tucked her hands under her arms, waiting for an invitation from him to come closer, maybe into the folds of his wool overcoat. But it wasn't coming.

"Are you going somewhere after this?" she tried.

"Yes. Big meeting of all the heads." He gazed over the river. "Likely they'll make my appointment permanent."

She nodded, looking at the ground. Yes, they probably would confirm him as the head of the Sava Syndicate. If there were any doubts before, there would be none now, after the way he dealt with the Red. In a way, she was proud of him, for tapping into the strength she knew was in him. But it was such a waste to use that power in that environment; for drugs, and rana, and intimidation, and all the things he didn't care about.

Theron broke the silence. "I wanted to - I mean, I meant to tell you something this morning."

Her heart was in her throat. She had no idea what might come out of his mouth.

"Thank you."

Surprised, she glanced up at him.

"Not for last night," he added in a hurry. "I mean everything before that. Bringing your family in to protect me. Putting your life on the line for me. No one has ever done that for me, not ever. I don't know why you would do such a thing. But I'll never forget it."

She stared at him, confused.

Then realization crawled over her.

He was cutting off contact. He was leaving.

A surge of anger burst through her, an eruption on the edge of her lips: *After everything I did for you, after last night and everything that's happened, now that it's finally resolved, you decide to end things?*

Then a heavy grief sank over her. She pushed her fists into her eyes, gathering her courage.

"Do you remember what you said to me, back in your house on the cliffs?" she began. "I asked you: why bother getting in touch with someone like me? Why bother with the effort?"

She smiled at the memory as she lowered her hands. "You told me: 'I think you have the potential to make a difference in the world.' I never forgot that. You planted the idea in my head that maybe I was more than a worthless outcast."

Theron's eyes shifted to the side. But he didn't speak, nor leave.

She wet her lips with her tongue, pushing out the words. "Theron, I don't care what different paths we're on, and I don't know how it would ever work, I just - I don't want to say good-bye. I don't -"

Theron turned his broad back to her.

She stared at the red cord that tied his hair back. Humiliation crept up her neck. Didn't he know how hard it was for her to be vulnerable?

No, she refused to let him reject her.

Phaira stepped forward, and rested her forehead on the center of his back. She let herself sink into the fabric, the smell of him, the warmth, willing him to turn around.

"I love you." The words tumbled out, slightly shrill, to her horror.

His reply was half carried away by the wind, but the clipped tone rang through. "Sorry, but I don't know what to tell you."

Phaira jerked away, as if electrocuted. Tears were building, stupid, embarrassing tears that she couldn't hold back. She couldn't believe what she'd heard.

I've never said that to anyone. And he rejected it.

Never again, she promised herself, as she ran up the hill, away from the sounds of the bridge. *I'll never say it again.*

* * *

The next day, Renzo was awake and mobile, but Sydel advised against him taking the controls of the *Arazura* just yet. Give it another day, she told him. Let CaLarca handle it.

CaLarca agreed. She got them into flight, and Renzo wandered and sat in random spots, grumbled about being an invalid again, and stole looks of jealousy at the cockpit. Sydel ignored him, as did Cohen. They were oddly restless, after all the frantic activity and danger. Nervous energy bounced off everyone. Except for Phaira, at least, as far as she could tell. She hadn't seen Phaira yet; CaLarca had lowered the *Arazura* on the outskirts of Lea so she could board, but the woman had gone directly into her cabin and shut the door. She must have been exhausted, Sydel reasoned, though a prickle of uncertainty came with that thought. There was something else going on, Sydel could sense it, but she wasn't going to push. Not yet.

"We need to leave."

Phaira appeared at the edge of her doorway. Her skin was sallow, her eyes glittering, and her dark mouth tight.

"Are you okay?" Cohen asked, staring at Phaira.

"Fine. We should get out of the East, and hide for a while.

"You think we're in danger?" Sydel asked, surprised.

"I'm not sure of anything," Phaira said curtly, "but we've been too exposed. Too many people know our faces and names. It's only going to get worse."

"So, where do we go? Back to Toomba?" Cohen asked hopefully.

"I will not," CaLarca's voice rang out. "I want to go West."

Phaira frowned. "West? To where?

"The border between Midland and the Kings," CaLarca said. There was a curious urgency in her voice.

"That's too far," Renzo said. "And there's nothing out there.

"Why do you want to go?" Phaira pushed, with a surprising level of bitterness. "Your friends out there?"

CaLarca flinched. She opened her mouth to say something, but her eyes averted, as if she were afraid.

Renzo sighed. "Look, Toomba's not my first choice either, but maybe it's -"

"No," CaLarca said darkly. "I won't go."

"You don't have a say," Phaira snapped.

The words hung in the air.

They were being unfair, Sydel knew it was true, but she made no move to correct it. They were in such a precarious position. They couldn't just fly into unknown territory. They needed somewhere safe, and guarded, until the storm passed.

But CaLarca's face was pinched and white, her eyes blacker than ever. Phaira lifted her chin at the woman, as if daring her to respond. Tension crackled between the women.

"Let's not decide right now," Renzo broke in. "We can talk about -"

Renzo stopped mid-sentence, and put a hand to the *Arazura* to steady himself.

Phaira and Cohen moved to help him. "What's wrong?" they asked simultaneously.

"Nothing, I just..." Renzo shook his head.

Then his eyes rolled into the back of his head, and he slumped against the paneling.

Phaira let out a cry of shock.

Then her body jerked, as if struck, and her body collapsed backwards in a blur of blue and white.

Cohen dropped to his knees, swiping at the air, before sprawling across the ground.

Sydel fought the swamping, willing her body to defend her, but she was so sluggish after the battle, and the urge to sleep was so insistent against her skull, pounding and pounding.

She couldn't hold the barrier up any longer.

The last thing she saw was CaLarca's livid face, her eyes swallowing her up in blackness.

about the author:

Born in Ontario, Canada, Loren Walker lives and works in Rhode Island. Her poetry has appeared in the anthologies <u>Routes,</u> Frequency Writers <u>City and Sea,</u> <u>The West Texas Review,</u> and <u>QU Journal</u>. Her debut novel EKO was a finalist in the Half the World Global Literary Award completion, chosen as a Library Journal SELF-e Select Pick, and a Shelf Unbound Notable Indie in 2016.

Get publishing updates, character biographies and custom illustrations at her official site: www.lorenwalker.net

The final book of the NINE Series is NYX.

thank you:

to my family and friends, my eternal cheerleaders.

to my beta reader Jill Corley, whose dramatic reactions always make me smile.

to my editor Lindsay Galloway, and to Deranged Doctor Design, for making INSYNN look good.

and to you, for buying this book.